PRAISE FOR ELEANOR & SAM

"Rachel Del Grosso is a gifted and natural storyteller whose debut is sure to please readers who enjoy layered novels about writing and women's relationships."

CAMILLE PAGÁN, BESTSELLING AUTHOR
OF *GOOD FOR YOU*

"I absolutely flew through this book. Compulsively readable and wholly satisfying, *Eleanor & Sam* is a love letter to authors, to books, to the creative process, to friendship—especially the unique, often tricky, bond that forms between artists. I loved every minute of it."

SUZY KRAUSE, BESTSELLING AUTHOR
OF *SORRY I MISSED YOU* AND *I THINK
WE'VE BEEN HERE BEFORE*

"A powerful story of two women and the choices they make that affect their lives forever. Two very different women bond over their love of story and how difficult it can be for women to find their way as writers in a world that still doesn't make it easy for creatives. A riveting page-turner you don't want to miss!"

JANUARY BAIN, AUTHOR OF THE *ANNA
HALE P.I.* SERIES

ANOTHER KIND OF GREEN

TITLES BY RACHEL DEL GROSSO

Eleanor & Sam

Fine, But Not Finished

ANOTHER KIND OF GREEN

RACHEL DEL GROSSO

To friends old and new

ANOTHER KIND OF GREEN

PROLOGUE

I stand at the kitchen sink, gripping the edge of the counter so hard my fingers ache. The hum of the dishwasher fills the silence, but it's not enough to drown out the clatter of plates left on the table or the sound of Anna's bedroom door slamming upstairs. It's just noise—background to the life I barely recognize anymore.

In the reflection of the window, I see myself. Tired eyes, dark circles that don't seem to go away no matter how much I sleep. I used to look happy. I used to feel *something*.

Now, I just feel numb.

Behind me, I hear Nick's slow and quiet footsteps, like he's not sure if he should even approach me. He doesn't say anything right away. He never does anymore. I can feel him there, hovering in the doorway, waiting for the right moment, as if it will somehow fix the gulf that's grown between us.

"You okay?" he finally asks. The words feel empty, like he's just saying them because he's supposed to.

"Yeah," I say automatically. "I'm fine."

I'm not fine. I haven't been fine in a long time, but I'm not sure I even know how to say it out loud anymore. We don't talk about real things these days, just the basics—who's picking up the kids, what bills are due, what we need from the grocery store. The important stuff, the things that *matter*, are buried under the surface.

Nick walks closer and places his hand on my shoulder, but it's more out of habit than affection. "I'll get the kids to bed," he says, his voice softer, distant. I nod, still staring at my reflection, at the tired woman staring back at me. I hear him walk away, but I don't follow him. I just stay here, anchored to this spot, gripping the counter like it's the only thing keeping me grounded.

This is how it happens, I think. This is how love fades. Not all at once. It slips away, moment by moment, day by day, until you don't even recognize the person standing next to you anymore.

Upstairs, I hear Anna's voice, muffled through the ceiling, and Ben's small footsteps heading down the hall. Their lives are still going, full of school, friends, and bedtime stories. All the things that used to make me feel alive, filling me with a sense of purpose and genuine connection to my kids' lives. Now, they just feel like tasks. One more thing I have to get done.

I close my eyes, squeezing the edge of the counter even harder. I want to believe it can get better, that Nick and I can find our way back to whatever it was we used to have. But when I think about how far we've drifted, it feels impossible, like I'm reaching across an ocean, and he's already too far away to hear me.

I open my eyes and see my reflection again. I don't know how much longer I can keep pretending this is enough. How much longer I can keep telling myself I'm fine.

CHAPTER
ONE

Like every other wife and mother in the history of the world I'm *tired*. Not the kind a good night's sleep can fix, but a deep, bone-weary exhaustion that has settled into every part of me. It's the kind of tired brought on by juggling too many roles and never feeling like I'm excelling at any of them. And like most mothers I know, there's no clear path to pulling myself out of this endless cycle of fatigue. I've simply learned to exist within the chaos. I accomplish this in a number of ways: by pretending a cartoon-covered Band-Aid can magically heal the invisible wounds my son carries from being the smallest kid in his class, and feigning disappointment at being too busy to attend my neighbor's daughter's graduation party, even though the thought of making small talk with a room full of strangers makes my skin crawl. I show displeasure when my husband mentions we haven't had sex in over two months, even though the mere idea of physical intimacy right now feels like another chore on my never-ending to-do list. I try to empathize deeply with my daughter's middle school dramas, recalling my own adolescent heartbreaks, though those memories feel distant and faded, like an old photograph left too long in the sun. I act as though turning forty in a few months doesn't bother me because age is just a number and not a ticking clock reminding me of all the dreams I have yet to fulfill.

I pretend I'm happy…which I most certainly am not.

These thoughts swirl in my mind as I sit in my car, parked in our cramped garage after the morning school drop-off. The engine ticks as it cools, filling the silence with a rhythmic reminder that time is passing, and I'm wasting it sitting here, hiding from my own life. Inside the house awaits a gauntlet of responsibilities I'm not ready to face just yet—a sink over-flowing with dirty dishes, baskets of laundry pleading to be folded, and a mountain of work emails.

My job as a managing editor for a small press book publisher has been my saving grace for the past ten years. Working from home allows me the flexibility to be present for my family, but it also blurs the lines between my profes-sional and personal life until there's no boundary left. Still, when I think back to all the books I've helped bring into the world from the small, cluttered desk crammed into the corner of my bedroom, I feel a surge of pride. In this space, amid the chaos, I'm competent, respected, and in control—feelings in short supply in the rest of my life.

I lean my head back against the headrest and close my eyes, allowing myself just a few more moments of solitude before stepping back into the fray. The garage smells faintly of gasoline and old paint, and the familiarity of the scents oddly comfort me. I consider turning the car back on and driving somewhere—anywhere—but I know it's just another fantasy. There's too much to do, too many people relying on me to simply run away.

With a resigned sigh, I grab my purse and push open the car door, only to have it smack directly into Ben's bike, which topples over with a loud clatter. The sound echoes sharply, amplifying my already frayed nerves. I clench my jaw, fighting the urge to scream, and bend down to pick up the tangled mess of metal and rubber. The chain has come loose, and grease smears across my already chipping manicure as I struggle to set it right.

"Perfect start to the day," I mutter under my breath, wiping my greasy hands on my jeans and making a mental note to remind Ben—again—to put his bike away properly.

Entering the house, I'm greeted by Mayer, our oversized gray Maine coon cat, weaving between my legs and meowing as if he hasn't been fed in days. A quick glance at his empty bowl confirms that Anna has neglected her one simple morning chore—again. Suppressing another sigh, I fill his bowl, watching as he dives into his food with gusto. At least someone in this house appreciates my efforts.

The kitchen is a disaster zone. Crumbs litter the countertops, and the sink is stacked high with breakfast dishes no one has thought to rinse, let alone load into the dishwasher. A sticky spill of orange juice glistens ominously on the floor threatening to catch me unaware later. I feel a familiar surge of frustration mixed with a hefty dose of resignation. Cleaning up after my family has become a Sisyphean task—no matter how much effort I put in, the mess always returns, usually within minutes.

I pour myself a generous cup of coffee and let the rich aroma soothe my frazzled nerves. The first sip is heaven, transporting me to a world where I'm not responsible for everyone and everything. Mug in hand, I make my way upstairs to my makeshift office, carefully stepping over the pile of dirty clothes strewn across the staircase landing. I debate whether to pick them up, but decide against it. If I don't start holding my ground, I'll drown under the weight of everyone else's expectations.

My office—or rather, the corner of our bedroom where

I've crammed a desk and a bookshelf—is the only space in the house that feels remotely mine. The walls are adorned with framed covers of books I've worked on, little tokens of accomplishment in a life that often feels devoid of personal achievement. I settle into my chair and wiggle the mouse to wake up my computer. The screen flickers to life, revealing an overflowing inbox filled with emails marked "urgent." At least here, among the chaos of deadlines and edits, I know what's expected of me.

Just as I begin to dive into the first email, my phone rings sharply, shattering the brief moment of peace. I glance at the caller ID—Ben's elementary school. My heart sinks as a dozen worst-case scenarios flash through my mind. I quickly answer, trying to keep the worry out of my voice.

"Good morning, this is Colette Dawson."

"Hi Mrs. Dawson, this is Ms. Reynolds from the front office. It seems Ben forgot his lunch today."

Of course he did.

I close my eyes, rubbing my temple with my free hand. "All right, I'll bring it over shortly."

"Thank you so much. Have a great day."

I hang up and let my head fall back against the chair, staring up at the ceiling as I contemplate the logistics of rearranging my already packed morning. I briefly consider letting him buy lunch from the cafeteria, but I know Ben hates the school food and would likely go hungry rather than eat it. With a groan, I push myself up from the chair and head back downstairs, abandoning any hope of getting an early start on work.

In the kitchen, I survey the sparse contents of our fridge and pantry, piecing together a makeshift lunch from a slightly bruised apple, a granola bar, and a hastily made peanut butter and jelly sandwich. It's not winning any nutrition awards, but it'll have to do. After grabbing my keys and the brown paper bag, I head back out, the unfinished coffee on my desk already growing cold.

———

Nick arrives home from work just as I'm setting dinner on the table. I took the time, on my lunch break, to chop the vegetables and prepare the chicken marinade so I could cook dinner more quickly later when I'm prone to running lower on energy—just one of the many tricks I've learned over the years. But I forgot to leave time for the sliced sweet potatoes to soak in water for thirty minutes before tossing them with olive oil and seasoning salt and throwing them into the air fryer, so they aren't as soft as they usually are; a fact that Anna points out to me after popping one into her mouth.

I shove three of the largest fries into my mouth to stop myself from responding.

A quick sideways glance at Ben tells me tonight is not going to be a night he'll eat his food without a fight. He's probably still on a sugar high from the Nutella sandwich, granola bar, and applesauce I threw together for his lunch this morning after realizing we were in desperate need of groceries.

There was no thank you for delivering his lunch to him— not that I was expecting one—but it would have been nice, for once, to be thanked for putting together a meal and cleaning their clothes and generally doing everything I can to keep them alive and well.

Being a mother really is a thankless job.

While the sweet potatoes are a bust, the chicken is moist and flavorful and the zucchini and broccoli are cooked perfectly—even if I'm the only one who's truly appreciating it as the rest of the family, Ben excluded, simply shovels it into their mouths like eating is just another thing to check off the to-do list rather than something to be slowly enjoyed.

"Ben, eat up," Nick says five minutes into dinner. Personally, I would have spoken up sooner, but I'm happy not to have had to be the one to bring it up first.

Ben responds with a grunt and begrudgingly stuffs a piece of broccoli into his mouth. I count the pieces of chicken and vegetables on his plate and, performing a quick calculation in my head, estimate I'll be sitting here with him for a total of twenty-seven more minutes while he eats. With the laundry still not done and some work I absolutely need to get done before the morning, I don't have the time to waste.

I note the time on the clock across the room. "Ben, I'm giving you ten minutes to eat or there's no more TV time tonight." This, naturally, elicits a loud groan. "Ten minutes," I repeat, more firmly this time.

Anna drops her fork on her plate and pushes it aside. "I'm done. Can I have my phone back now?"

Nick and I recently instituted a no phones at the table rule after it became clear we were talking to one another less and less. I wish I could say Anna was the worst offender, but Nick and I weren't much better. There was always one more work email to respond to, or, in my case, an inner office communication message demanding my attention. Now, we have to leave our cell phones in an entirely different room where we can't be tempted by the beeps and dings and whistles. Some days we're great about talking to each other, and other days, like tonight, it seems as though we're all off in our own worlds. We're...whatever the absolute opposite of present is.

With Anna off and reunited with her phone, it's just the three of us. Ben is staring down at his plate with a scowl on his face that could be seen from the moon—any chance at conversation with him is off the table. Which leaves only Nick.

"How was work today?" I ask. Granted, it's not the most unique of conversation starters, but I have to start somewhere.

His sigh is heavy, loaded. "Brutal, honestly." He pushes back from the table and takes his and Anna's dishes to the dishwasher. "I'm tired of babysitting grown men all day, and Will is of little to no help lately."

"I'm sorry," I say, because what else is there to say? It's not like I can physically do anything to help his situation. It's all part of the job, as far as I'm concerned, like how I have to deal with my share of nit-picky, overly involved authors in my job. Life is all about balancing the bad with the good. He knows that as well as I do.

He does look tired though. And he certainly looks as though he could use a long, hot shower.

"Go get cleaned up," I tell him. "I'll make sure Ben eats."

And then there are two.

Across the street, my best friend Zoey and her family are probably sitting down to dinner, too. But unlike what's happening here, they're probably having a spirited discussion about something her twins learned in school today, or contemplating where their next family vacation will take them. Meanwhile, we haven't been outside of Nevada in over three years, not since our road trip to La Jolla not long before COVID rocked the world.

I try not to compare our lives—it isn't fair to either of us— but on days like today, it's hard not to notice the disparities. Zoey has the bigger house, the successful husband who adores her, the kids who excel at everything they try. Meanwhile, I'm struggling to keep my head above water, my marriage feels stagnant, and my kids are…well, kids.

I set my elbows on the table and rest my chin in my hands, watching Ben pop the second-to-last piece of zucchini into his mouth. Upstairs, Nick is showering, and Anna is surely zoning out watching TikTokers apply makeup. I'm alone with my thoughts—the worst thing for someone like me.

Later, in bed, I stare up at the dark ceiling, unable shake the feeling something needs to change. I'm tired of settling for a life that feels like a series of obligations rather than something I actively chose. I don't know the answer or how to find it, but for the first time in a long time, I allow myself to acknowledge the dissatisfaction simmering beneath the surface. I allow myself to wonder if there's a way for things to change that doesn't involve blowing up my life as I know it.

CHAPTER
TWO

Nick and I met fourteen years ago, introduced by a mutual friend who's no longer in our lives, for reasons none of us can quite pinpoint. This friend, who had known us both for most of our lives, thought we might be a good match when he saw us across the room at a party. I remember catching sight of Nick from across the crowded space, and something about the way he carried himself drew me in immediately. It sounds cliché, but at that moment, I knew I would marry him. It took Nick a little longer to reach the same conclusion, but once he did, we became inseparable.

Back then, I was a doe-eyed twenty-five-year-old with big dreams of working in publishing, but in the wrong city to do so. New York was out of the question—I couldn't see myself thriving in such a frantic city. Nashville, Denver, San Francisco—they all held promise, but none of them felt like home. Las Vegas was in my blood, and despite the odds, I was determined to build a life and a career here. I applied for every publishing-related job I could find: proofreader, copywriter, editorial assistant, literary agent—anything to get my foot in the door. I was relentless, and eventually, my determination paid off. A publisher in New York wanted to establish a presence on the West Coast, and while I wasn't exactly in LA, I was close enough. I was in.

Nick's journey was different. Though he was only two years older, he seemed miles ahead in life. He'd started working in construction during high school, spending weekends and summers learning the trade. He knew where his path was leading him, so he bypassed college and went straight into the workforce, earning both a contractor's license and a property management license. By the time I met him, he had already started his own company with his best friend, Will, specializing in commercial construction and property management. He was house shopping, building his empire.

Within weeks of meeting, we were a couple, effortlessly blending our lives as if we'd been together for years. Nick started bringing me along to look at houses, valuing my opinion on properties that could have been our future home. It didn't matter to me whether we ended up in a one-bedroom apartment or a sprawling two-story in Summerlin—I just wanted to be where he was.

The day he signed the closing papers on his new house, he carried me over the threshold, set me down, and dropped to one knee to propose. Six months later, we were married in the backyard, surrounded by our closest friends and family. I wore a strapless chiffon off-white gown, and Nick wore a gray linen suit. As he promised to love me through thick and thin, in sickness and in health, I remember feeling a profound certainty that nothing in our lives would ever be difficult again.

Back then, I didn't have to feign happiness.

———

This morning, determined to start the day on the right foot, I woke up early enough to enjoy my first cup of coffee alone in silence, savoring the rare peace that only comes with the dawn. By the time the rest of the house began to stir, I had already prepared the kids' lunches—ham and cheese sandwiches (one with mayo, one with mustard), cucumber slices, pretzels, and the requisite sugary snack thrown in for good measure. I even managed to prep my own semblance of a healthy breakfast and fold a load of laundry sitting in a basket at the foot of my bed for three days. For a fleeting moment, I felt like I might actually have my life under control.

But of course, life had other plans. As I poured a second cup of coffee into a to-go container for the school drop-off, the carafe slipped from my hand, sending a cascade of coffee across the counter and onto my pants. I stood there for a moment, watching the dark liquid spread, feeling the familiar sting of frustration.

Life: 1, Colette: 0.

Even as I mopped up the mess, I couldn't stop myself from mentally comparing my chaotic start to the day with Zoey's across the street. Her husband, Aaron, despite being one of the busiest guys I know, somehow always has time to help get the kids ready for school. I imagined him preparing a breakfast more involved than dumping cereal into a bowl, maybe even cooking something nutritious and Instagram-worthy. The kids probably drink almond milk or oat milk in their cereal—Zoey banned dairy from their household after reading one too many alarming studies linking it to all sorts of health issues. The Adler household is a paragon of modern health-conscious living, right down to their organic, non-GMO snacks.

Zoey and Aaron probably had sex this morning too—quietly, so as not to wake the kids. I can't recall the last time

Nick and I managed anything remotely spontaneous. Ben might still have been a baby.

I try not to dwell on it, but sometimes it's hard not to let these thoughts creep in. Zoey thinks I'm stuck in the past, trying to hold on to a time before kids and all the responsibilities that come with them. She tells me constantly that the only way to reignite my sex life is to think outside the box more.

I don't have the heart to tell her I'm too tired to think outside of anything—box, circle, hexagon, whatever.

She loves giving me unsolicited advice about my marriage, and while I used to find it annoying, I'd probably have stopped going to her with my problems if it really did bother me. Her advice, though well-intentioned, always feels a little too simplistic, like when I texted her last week in a fit of frustration, venting about Nick not pulling his weight at home.

The grass is greener where you water it, she replied.

I never did respond to her text.

—————

As soon as I sign onto Slack, our inner office communication program, the messages start pouring in, the *beeping* and *booping* of notifications threatening to drown out my morning caffeine buzz. My assistant tells me she'll be in late—again. The Art Director asks for feedback on a cover design for one of our upcoming young adult fantasy titles. But the message requiring my immediate attention is from my colleague, Emily, who sends her weekly photo of her growing baby daughter. This week, the baby is seated in a pocket of sunlight, grinning madly at the camera. I rattle off an obligatory "awww" followed by a slew of emojis, feeling a pang of nostalgia as I remember the days when my own kids were that little. Those years seem so far away now, like a different life altogether. The back-breaking exhaustion, the endless diaper changes, the constant worry—it's a miracle I made it through as well as I did. Emily's baby is adorable, but I have no desire to relive those newborn years—whether with Nick or anyone else.

After one last look at the photo, I take a deep breath and settle in to begin my workday. Publishing is a satisfying career; there's something deeply gratifying about seeing a project through from conception to completion, holding the final product in your hands. Making an author's dreams come true—it's the kind of reward that keeps you going, even on the most stressful days. Each day in publishing is different. Monday might be spent responding to author emails, Tuesday in meetings with the art team discussing cover designs, Wednesday onboarding new authors and attending team meetings, and Thursday and Friday buried in edits, compiling metadata, and planning social media strategies. The work is always challenging, always varied, and rarely boring. It's easy to see how my efforts translate into real, tangible results— proof I'm good at what I do.

In contrast, parenting feels like a never-ending marathon with no clear finish line. Years of hard work, with no guarantee your efforts will pay off in any visible way. So far, all Nick and I have to show for our efforts are one child who might just be the world's pickiest eater and another who's perfecting the pre-teen sneer of disgust. I do love them though; don't get me wrong.

The muted ring of an incoming call shakes me from my thoughts. On my screen, my boss, Brent, is calling me into a huddle. I click "Join," and his unshaven face fills the screen. I glance at the small window reflecting my own image back at me, noting the unmade bed in the background with a groan. Too late to do anything about it now, so I ignore it and hope he does too.

"Morning, Colette." His voice is unusually raspy, almost as if he'd just woken up, but Brent is a creature of habit, up at five every morning without fail.

"Good morning," I echo, trying to sound cheerful.

"Do you have a few minutes to talk through some things?" He adjusts the well-worn baseball cap on his head.

"I do." I have another meeting in an hour, leaving plenty of time to discuss whatever he needs.

"Great." He settles back in his chair. "I've been thinking about doing a little restructuring, maybe shifting some people around to roles where they're better suited."

I know from years of experience that it's best to let Brent talk through his ideas before offering any input. "Okay."

"What would you think about having Emily manage the young adult imprint and moving Matt to thrillers? I know Matt's been doing a good job, but I think Emily could really take things to the next level."

In my mind, there's no question. Besides being the youngest and one of the smartest members of our team, Emily has a natural enthusiasm that would serve her well in young adult fiction. "Emily would be perfect for the YA titles. I actually wish we'd thought of it sooner. Plus, Matt's versatile—he'll do well anywhere."

Brent nods, looking relieved. "Glad to hear it. I wasn't sure if it was just another harebrained idea, or if it had legs."

"It's a great idea," I reassure him. "We just need to figure out the best timing for the transition. Have you spoken to Emily about it yet? Is she interested in managing young adult titles?"

"I wanted to get your take on it first. But maybe you could gauge her interest? The two of you could come up with a plan for the transition."

"The three of us, you mean?"

Brent pauses before answering. "Maybe just the two of you for now. Let's not involve Matt just yet."

His hesitation gives me pause—there's something he isn't telling me, but I know better than to press. "Okay. I'll talk to Emily and keep Matt out of it for now."

The huddle ends, and I'm left staring at my desktop wallpaper—a rare photo of Nick, the kids, and me, all smiling at the camera. It was taken by my mother-in-law on my thirty-eighth birthday the year before. I try not to focus on the fine lines spreading across my forehead or the deepening frown line between my eyebrows, a gift from my mother's side of the family. There's no escaping it—I'm getting older. Forty is looming on the horizon—not yet old, but no longer young.

When I was younger, I had so many ideas of what my life would look like by the time I reached forty. But as I sit here, reflecting on the past, I realize how far off the mark I've veered. The extra twenty pounds around my middle, the anxiety over meal planning, the lack of spontaneity in my marriage—none of it matches the picture I once painted in my mind. And as much as I try to avoid the comparison, I can't help but think of Zoey. She seems to have it all: the successful career, the perfect marriage, the well-behaved kids. And if the looks I often catch her and Aaron exchanging are any indication, she's having the kind of hot, spontaneous sex I once imagined I'd be having.

Would Nick ever look at me that way again?

CHAPTER
THREE

I'm sitting on the couch for not more than ten minutes, Mayer curled up against my hip, when Nick comes through the front door, well after nine. The lights are off, more out of neglect than intent, but I make no move to alert him to my presence either. It's no surprise, then, when he yelps after spotting me in the dim room. Before I can think better of it, I shush him, not wanting to wake the kids. Ben fought sleep with the kind of stubbornness only young children can muster, and I'm not ready to face his bleary-eyed protests again.

Nick shoots me a look as he passes by, heading straight for the kitchen. I know his routine by heart—he'll pour himself a tall glass of cold water to take with him to bed, a habit he's had for as long as I can remember. Glass in hand, he soon returns, hovering over me in the way only he knows how to do, his presence filling the space between us.

His eyes scan the room, taking in the mess that's accumulated throughout the day—Ben's toys and LEGOs strewn across the floor, Anna's stuffed animals scattered on the couch, my work notes spread haphazardly across the coffee table. I can practically see the gears turning in his head, calculating the chaos.

"It's gotten a little crazy in here," he says, his tone neutral, carefully choosing his words to avoid sounding accusatory.

I look up at him, feeling a flicker of irritation. Mayer, perhaps sensing the energy shift, abandons his spot beside me and pads away. "What do you expect, Nick? There's no room in this place anymore. We've completely outgrown it."

Nick sighs, the weight of the day settling onto his shoulders. "Do we really have to get into this now? I just got home, and I'm exhausted. Couldn't you pick a better time to bring this up?"

"I didn't bring up anything," I shoot back, my voice low to avoid waking the kids. "You started this conversation."

"Whatever, I'm going to bed," he mutters, already turning away.

"We need a bigger place, Nick." I watch him round the bottom of the stairs, my frustration bubbling over. "You can ignore it all you want, but you know I'm right."

His footsteps pause for a fraction of a second before continuing up the stairs, his silence louder than any words he could have spoken.

———

The next morning, after dropping the kids off at school, I take a detour. Not to grab a takeout coffee—though the thought crosses my mind—but to visit the model home that's become my sanctuary. It isn't caffeine, but it always leaves me feeling reenergized, a small escape from the cramped reality of our current living situation.

The woman at the sales office knows me by name now, a testament to how many times I've come by. She's on the phone when I walk in but greets me with a nod and a knowing smile. I return the smile, already feeling the familiar sense of excitement bubbling up as I head toward the model home.

From the moment you open the double doors, it's perfection. The foyer welcomes you with three choices: head to the laundry room on the left, two bedrooms and a bathroom on the right, or continue down the hall past a small den into the great room, featuring a white, airy kitchen that makes me want to take up baking. Beyond the kitchen is a small café room nestled into the far back corner, light streaming in from the glass door leading to the backyard. Opposite the kitchen is a short hallway leading to the master bedroom and bathroom, both pristine and spacious.

It's my dream house. And there's standing inventory available.

In all the times I've walked through this model, I've never brought Nick with me. At first, it was just curiosity, a way to pass the time and indulge in a little harmless fantasy. But as the months went on, I began to wonder if moving could be a real option. The price is right, within our range, and the location is perfect—only two miles from our current place, which means school pickups and drop-offs wouldn't be affected. The new house would even put us closer to the beltway, shaving a few minutes off Nick's commute.

I start to fantasize about the house daily, imagining myself in each room, envisioning a life where there's space to breathe, where the clutter of our current home is replaced by sleek, organized storage. I'm obsessed, and I know it. But I also know I'm willing to do just about anything to get what I want.

Back in my car, I send Nick a text:

> Can the guys start without you
> tomorrow? I want to show you
> something. I only need twenty minutes.

It's time to introduce my husband to my newest love.

———

It doesn't take long to recognize Nick doesn't share my enthusiasm for the model home. In fact, he's downright nit-picky, which isn't like him at all. If I didn't know better, I'd think he'd made up his mind to dislike it before he even stepped through the door. What I see as clean and minimalis-tic, he sees as empty and cold. Where I see natural light streaming through the windows, he sees too many panes of glass needing expensive coverings. The three-car garage I consider a necessity (*Hello*, I can barely open my car door without taking out a children's bicycle), he deems excessive—never mind we can barely fit my mid-sized car and his work truck in our current garage. I sometimes end up parking on the street just to avoid the hassle.

"I know it might be hard to picture ourselves here with all this furniture and stuff," I say, trying to keep my voice even. "We could ask to look at some of the standing inventory houses? They'd be empty, so it might be easier to imagine our things in the space."

"I have to go," Nick says, glancing at his watch. He takes one last slow look around the great room before his gaze meets mine. "It's…an idea."

I'm not ready to give up. "Another time, then."

A small sigh escapes his lips, barely audible. "Moving is a pain, Colette. And new houses are expensive. Plus, our house is all the kids know. I like the idea of watching them grow up there."

"I get it," I say, following him out to his truck. "It all sounds nice, but it's also true we need more space. There's no storage in our house, Nick. And I'm working from the bedroom, which wasn't a big deal at first, but now I'm spending more time on calls with authors and it's awkward."

He pauses, his hand on the door handle. "We can make it work; I just need some time to think," he says, his tone more final than I like.

"I don't know what that means," I say. A knot of frustration tightens in my chest.

"We'll renovate, make more storage," he says as if it's so simple.

Renovate? Is he serious? I can practically feel my heart rate increasing. "Can you renovate an extra thousand square feet out of thin air?"

His mouth hardens into a straight line, and he glances at his watch again. "I really have to go."

"Why are you being like this?" My voice wavers, a mix of desperation and hurt.

He exhales sharply. "I'm not trying to be anything; I just really have to go. Will..." He trails off, leaving the sentence unfinished, as if I can fill in the blanks myself.

"Fine," I mutter, turning away from him before he can see the disappointment etched on my face.

All I ask for is twenty minutes of his time to look at a potential solution to our housing problem, and he can barely oblige. Maybe the next time he comes sliding over onto my side of the bed, looking for time and attention, I'll give him as little as he gives me today. Which is to say, pretty much nothing at all.

I sit in my car long after he drives away, staring longingly out the window at the line of houses I'll probably have to kiss goodbye before I fall even more in love with them.

Nick can't possibly be serious about renovating our house. Sure, it could use some updating—fresh paint on the walls, an upgraded kitchen, and maybe a new banister to replace the outdated one—but none of it would change the ultimate problem: we need more space. And when exactly are these renovations going to take place? Nick's schedule is packed as it is, and if he plans to do the work himself, it'll probably take years. No, it doesn't make sense—not as much as starting fresh somewhere new and bigger.

Strangely enough, when I fill Zoey in on my predicament later that night, she seems to side with Nick. It's not like I expect my best friend to agree with me on everything, but this house issue seems like a no-brainer.

"Is this all because you want to keep me across the street?" I ask, only half-joking. "You know two miles is nothing."

With the kids occupied upstairs and the men off doing their own thing, Zoey and I are free to indulge in a little wine. I try to ignore the remnants of broccoli on the counter as I slide her glass across the table. I sincerely hope she hasn't noticed the mess.

"I absolutely want you to stay across the street," she says, taking a sip. "Two miles might as well be two states away as far as I'm concerned. I like having you close by."

The thought crosses my mind that if we move, I won't have to see her and Aaron smiling and flirting as they unload groceries or catch a glimpse of him shirtless in the yard pulling weeds. The latter is more my guilty conscience speaking than anything else—Aaron is definitely the kind of guy you can't help but look at, shirtless or not.

I swear I used to look at Nick like that at one point...

"I don't have a choice, Zo. Look at this place"—I swing my arm around dramatically—"We're bursting at the seams."

"But there are ways to fix that. Nick's a contractor; I'm sure he's worked miracles like this before."

Ok, scratch what I said earlier—I *absolutely* want Zoey to take my side over Nick's every single time. "Our life is already a mess. Why on earth would I want to add renovating a house while living in it to the madness?"

Zoey puts her hands up in mock surrender. "All right, all right. I get it. I swear I just—" Her phone chimes, cutting her off. She glances down at the screen, and a smile spreads across her face. "It's Aaron. He wants me to come right home."

The smile on her face makes me sick with envy.

"Totally a booty call," I say, forcing a grin.

She sips back her glass, finishing the wine in one gulp. "The twins?"

I nod. "They're good to stay."

"You're the best friend a girl could have!" she calls, dashing out the door with a wave.

———

Nick appears in the kitchen shortly after Zoey leaves, dropping a yellow legal pad and pen on the counter beside me. I sip my wine, bracing myself for whatever's coming next.

"I love this house, and I know you do too," he begins, his tone measured. "Our kids were born here, it has too many memories to just up and leave when things get uncomfortable." Here, I can't help but think he's talking about something other than the house, but I keep the thought to myself. "So I want you to think about what you might need to stay."

He taps the pad of paper with his finger. "Write a list. Anything and everything you want to change about this house. Then we can go over it together."

From the corner of the room, my phone begins to play "Good As Hell" by Lizzo—my ringtone for Zoey. I let it ring.

Nick has said his piece, and now it's my turn. "What did you think of the house this morning?"

He sucks in his bottom lip, considering his words. "It was fine. But like I said, I think we can make it work here. You just have to have a little faith in me."

"It's not about faith," I say, meaning it. "I just think there's no way around not enough space, no matter how we spin it."

My phone rings again—Good As Hell. I frown. Shouldn't she be deep under the covers with Aaron by now?

I apologize to Nick and make a mad dash for my phone. Zoey starts talking before I can even say hello.

I listen for a moment, confusion creeping in as her words tumble out in a frantic rush. "Whoa, whoa. Slow down. What—"

She's so hysterical I can barely understand her. I hear her pause and take a deep breath. Her next words are as clear as day.

"My marriage...I—it's over."

CHAPTER
FOUR

I make it to Zoey's door in record time. She answers with tears streaming down her face, her usually bright and confident demeanor reduced to something unrecognizable. Her face is blotchy and red, her eyes swollen from crying. Without a word, I follow her into the living room, where she sinks heavily onto the couch. My heart pounds unevenly in my chest as I sit down beside her, unsure of what to say, unsure of anything at this moment.

"What...I..." I stammer, my voice barely audible. For thirty-nine years, I've prided myself on always having the right words, the perfect response for any situation. But now, when I need them most, they fail me. I'm speechless, grasping for something—anything—that might make this better.

"Aaron's cheating on me," Zoey says, her voice flat, devoid of the energy I usually associate with her. It feels like the air has been sucked out of the room, leaving me light-headed and disoriented. My first instinct is to shake my head, to tell her it can't possibly be true. Aaron lives and breathes for his family. He adores Zoey. There's just no way this could be real.

"Say more," my brain whispers, echoing the phrase my

therapist likes to use in our monthly sessions, but I remain frozen, paralyzed by the weight of the revelation. Instead, I reach over and squeeze Zoey's hand in mine, hoping that the simple gesture can communicate what I can't put into words.

"It's been going on for two years. Two years," she repeats, her voice breaking on the last word.

"Who?" I whisper, the question barely escaping my lips.

"I didn't ask. I didn't want to know."

"What do you mean you don't want to know? Don't you have a thousand questions? I mean…don't you just want to murder him?"

Her eyes meet mine, and I see a deep, overwhelming sadness there. "I'm too sad to be angry."

"Give it time," I mutter under my breath. I squeeze her hand even tighter, my mind racing with questions I don't dare voice. "So what—what now?"

"I told him to get out."

———

Zoey has always been the kind of person who can find joy in the small, everyday moments of life—at least that's the impression I got the first time I laid eyes on her across a grocery store parking lot. I was packing groceries into my trunk when I heard the distinct sound of female laughter. I looked up to see a young woman pushing a cart with one toddler seated in the front while she balanced a second on her hip. Both kids have chocolate smeared across their faces, their expressions lit up with unbridled joy. I watched as she leaned down, her mouth also covered in chocolate, and kissed first the baby in her arms, then the one in the cart. They howled with laughter, and I found myself smiling at the sheer delight in their voices.

As they approached, I was transfixed. It was a rare afternoon when I was alone, without Anna, and I couldn't resist offering to help her with her groceries. She introduced herself as Zoey—of course, she would have such a cool name—and accepted my offer as she tried to clean the mess from her twins' faces. I had to remind her, with a smile matching hers, that her face also needed some cleaning. The weather was gorgeous, a perfect fall day, and we found ourselves standing next to her car, talking long after her kids were cleaned up and the groceries were piled away.

Her twins, Sam and Stella, were thirteen months old, just a month older than Anna. Zoey and her husband Aaron had recently moved to Las Vegas from California, drawn by the promise of more space and lower taxes. What neither of us could have anticipated was that they were the family who had just moved in across the street from Nick and me. It had been a whirlwind of a move appearing to happen overnight—one day, the house was for sale, and the next, it was occupied.

We made plans to get the kids together later that day, and as we drove home—down the same streets, following the same route—I remember feeling as though a piece of my life had finally clicked into place. It wasn't that I didn't have other friends, because I did, and some of them even had young kids. But none of them, no matter how long they'd been in my life, had made me feel the way Zoey did, like I could truly be myself. The feeling was mutual.

Zoey, Aaron, Nick, and I became fast friends. I was thrilled to see Nick hit it off with another guy—he had always been one of those men who spent more time in the company of women than men, which had always left me feeling a little insecure. For years, I worried one of his female friends would suddenly confess to having been in love with him all along, and Nick would run off into the sunset with her. My thoughts aren't always rational, but they're persistent.

After ten years of friendship, I like to think I know Zoey

and Aaron pretty well. I've witnessed the growth of their marriage over the years, and seen them through the ups and downs all couples face. But one thing has always remained constant—the way Aaron looks at Zoey. It's a look of love and adoration any woman would kill for.

So I'm shocked when Zoey admits to me, on this cold night in March, that Aaron has been having an affair for the past two years. Zoey and Aaron have always been my #relationshipgoals. If they can't make it, what does it mean for the rest of us? What does it mean for Nick and me?

————

I try to focus on what Zoey is saying, but it's hard to separate her thoughts from my own. Words like trust, love, and guilt swirl around in my mind, mingling with my own fears and insecurities until I can hardly tell fact from fiction.

"I know I don't have any right to say this," I finally manage, my voice trembling, "but I just don't understand. He just...told you he was having an affair?"

Zoey has stopped crying for the moment, her face a mask of exhaustion. "The text he sent me, wanting me to come home? It was so we could talk. So he could tell me he's been seeing someone else. That he's in love with someone else. Eve, he said her name is."

"Eve? Ew." The words slipping out before I can stop them.

A small smile breaks through Zoey's tears. "Ew?"

I drop my head into my hands, embarrassed. "I don't know what I'm saying."

"You should have seen him, Letty. He was so calm. He just sat me down right here on the couch, and out it came. His voice didn't even waver." She pulls in a shaky breath. "He said he couldn't keep it from me any longer."

"What does he want to do? I mean..."

"He said he still loves me and wants to be with me."

"Is he still seeing her?"

"I didn't ask."

"Zoey!" I exclaim, unable to keep the frustration out of my voice.

She seems to shrink further into the couch. "I was in shock. The whole thing was over in six minutes. The second the word 'love' came into the conversation, I told him to leave. I couldn't look at him anymore."

It's not possible. There's no way Aaron can look at Zoey the way he does, kiss her and adore her the way he does, and love someone else at the same time. And his children—he loves the twins, it's obvious just how much in every interaction he has with them. He would never risk hurting them like this. No, I refuse to believe this isn't all just some big mistake and he'll come to his senses. Zoey just needs to give him some time, to be patient and forgiving, and he'll come back where he's meant to be. Home is where he's meant to be. You always find your way back to the place you belong.

"What are you thinking? Now that you've had a little bit of time to process everything?" Even as the words leave my mouth, I know how ridiculous they sound. An hour is hardly enough time to process something this big. "You must feel so blindsided." I know I do.

Zoey is quiet for a while before speaking. "We weren't perfect, you know."

Her tone carries a hint of annoyance, and I find myself wanting to shrink into the couch as well. "I know."

"We had our issues. I sound like every other bored housewife when I say he worked too much, but it's true. And I'm awful to admit this, but I felt like he paid more attention to the twins than to me."

I want to dispute this, to tell her she's wrong, but I keep my mouth shut.

"We weren't talking like we used to," she continues. "That's always how it starts, isn't it?"

That's certainly how me and Nick's problems seemed to start.

"And we weren't having sex like we used to either. Or as often."

My heart pounds in my chest. This is all starting to sound a little too familiar, hitting too close to home.

I can't keep my thoughts to myself any longer. "This can't be right, what with all the stories you've told me. Just last week, you said you two didn't even make it home from dinner. Remember? You hurt your neck hitting the—"

"I lied," she interrupts, her voice barely above a whisper.

I still. "Why?"

"You've always had this idea about me and Aaron, right from the beginning, and I never wanted to tell you anything that would make you change your mind about us. I loved the way you saw us. I wanted us to still be that couple." Her mouth opens as though she's going to say more, but she hesitates, and then falls silent.

I close my eyes, exhaling slowly. "I wish you'd told me you guys were having trouble. All the times I complained about Nick...You could have told me, Zo."

"I know and I'm sorry."

I can't stop shaking my head, disbelief clouding my thoughts. "But still—an affair? I just can't believe it. Never in a million years."

Tears resume running down Zoey's face. "It wasn't as big of a shock as you think."

I reach for her hand again, my face screwed up in confusion. "What do you mean?"

"The truth is, I've been worried for a while that something was going on."

My mouth falls open. "You mean that he was having an affair?"

She nods so imperceptibly I almost miss it. "And I didn't do a damn thing about it."

CHAPTER
FIVE

Many hours and glasses of wine later, I finally manage to calm Zoey down enough she falls asleep. I gently pull a blanket over her on the couch, then set a cold glass of water and a fresh box of Kleenex within reach. For a moment, I just stand there, watching her breathe, her face finally at peace after the emotional storm she's weathered. Then, I quietly creep upstairs to check on the twins.

Both are sound asleep in their rooms, looking like the angels they are during the day. I can't fathom what Aaron's betrayal will mean for them, and for their family. How could two children who are so loved and cared for suddenly be thrust into the chaos of a fractured home? I can only hope after whatever happens, Zoey and Aaron will do everything in their power to make it as easy on the twins as possible.

I close their doors quietly and, with one final glance at Zoey's sleeping form, I step out of the house, locking the door behind me. Standing on the front porch, I look out at the familiar street, now cloaked in darkness. The stillness of the night contrasts sharply with the turmoil churning inside me. No matter what happens behind closed doors, I can't imagine putting my kids through a separation, or worse, a divorce. I know it's sometimes necessary, it can even work out for the best, but that won't be us. It can't be.

When I finally crawl into bed beside Nick, he's already asleep, but he soon stirs, rolling over to face me. His voice is thick with sleep. "Is she okay?"

I shake my head slightly, though I know he can't see it in the dark. "No, but she will be. I'll make sure of it."

"What is Aaron thinking?" he murmurs, disbelief tinged with anger in his voice.

I reach out and place my hand on his forearm, a gesture that feels oddly foreign. It doesn't escape me that this is the first time in a long while I've willingly touched him. "He told her he's in love with this other woman. But he also said he's still in love with Zoey and wants to be with her."

Nick puts his hand on top of mine, a silent offering of comfort. "Then they'll work it out. You'll see," he says with a sigh. "It's late, you should get some rest."

What I want him to say is that he'll get up with the kids in the morning, and he'll take care of breakfast and get them off to school. I want him to tell me to sleep in. He'll handle everything, just this once. But of course, he doesn't.

Life: 2, Colette: 0.

———

The next morning, sleep, a healthy breakfast, and a large cup of coffee bring no relief. In fact, everything feels worse in the harsh light of day. Not only have I been unable to sleep in, I wake up to find Nick has already left for work, leaving a hastily scribbled note on the kitchen counter: *Something came up. See you tonight.* I imagine, just for a moment, what it might be like to leave a note of my own and run off, leaving him to deal with everything by himself.

I tell the kids to pour their own cereal for breakfast because I have to run across the street to check on something.

Zoey is still in the same spot on the couch when I let myself in through the front door. We exchanged keys long ago, ostensibly for emergency purposes, though we use them far more regularly. The twins are awake, of course, and in the kitchen, eating breakfast. Is that—Yes, they've made themselves scrambled eggs. Color me impressed.

I wave at the kids, then move closer to Zoey. "Zo?"

Her eyes are red and swollen, her face splotchy. She looks like a shadow of herself, all the light and energy drained from her. "I can tell by the face you're making I look fabulous, just as expected," she says, her voice rough.

I manage a small smile. "You're making jokes—that's a good sign."

"Only to mask my pain," she replies, her tone flat.

I glance toward the kitchen. "Do they know what's going on?" I ask gently.

"Of course not. I don't want to scare them." Her expression darkens as she looks up at me. "Or should I tell them? So they don't feel like I'm keeping secrets from them too? I don't want them to think they can't trust me."

My shoulders slump. "I don't know, hon. I think maybe you should talk to Aaron. He—"

"I will not be consulting with him about this. He lost the right the moment he stuck his dick in someone else." She says this loudly enough I cast a quick glance up at the kids to see if they've heard. Thankfully, they seem engrossed in their breakfast, which now as I look closer, includes bacon. Say what you want about their marriage, Aaron and Zoey have raised some impressively independent children. I'm lucky if my kids can manage to pour their own milk into their cereal without spilling half of it.

I sit down on the floor at her feet, my heart aching for her.

"He's still their dad," I say softly, hoping my words won't set her off. There's a part of me that fears she might lash out, that her grief might turn into anger directed at anyone who dares to defend Aaron. But when she looks at me, there's no fight in her eyes, only a deep, hollow sadness. Aaron has done a number on her, this much is clear.

I take a deep breath, trying to steady myself. "What can I do? Can I take the kids to school?"

Zoey pulls her legs up and tucks them under her, a small sigh escaping her lips. "Would you mind?"

"Of course not." I stand up quickly, grateful to have something tangible to do, something actually helpful. "Stella, Sam," I call into the kitchen, "I'm taking you to school today, so just come over to my house at the usual time and we'll head out."

"I call back seat!" Sam hollers. I have to smile; most kids would have called shotgun, but Sam has ulterior motives. He always loves having the back seat to himself, free to sprawl out and daydream.

I turn back to Zoey. "I'll check in on you later, okay? Try to take a shower when the kids leave—it'll help. And drink lots of water. You need to hydrate after all that crying last night." I bend over and kiss her on the head, a gesture of reassurance as much for myself as for her. "Talk soon."

Back at my house, my kids are no closer to being ready for school than when I left them. At least they've managed to eat breakfast. I ask Anna to please get her bag packed, then have to cajole Ben into his bedroom to get dressed and brush his teeth. His homework from the night before is still on the kitchen table, and I have to remind him to pack it in his bag. The kid is so hyper-focused on everything except what he's supposed to be doing that he'd probably forget to put on underwear if I didn't constantly poke and prod him. Whatever Zoey and Aaron are doing with their kids, I need lessons—stat.

It's no small miracle I have everyone packed into the car on time. There will be no racing through yellow lights or rolling through stop signs this morning, which is a relief. One of these days, my luck is going to run out. Stella takes the front seat, happily commandeering the music playlist, while Sam, Anna, and Ben squeeze into the back, their backpacks resting on their laps. Ben looks miserable, as usual, but Anna and Sam are deep in a hushed conversation, their faces lit up with their usual cheerfulness. I do my best to commit their smiles to memory, not wanting this moment, this day, to end. Not wanting their happiness to end. Whatever Zoey and Aaron decide, they need to do whatever they can to keep those smiles on their children's faces.

The carpool line is a zoo despite us arriving on time. As I inch the car forward at a snail's pace, my thoughts drift from school drop-off to the plans for my day, to the strong desire for more coffee, the kitchen that still needs to be cleaned, and finally landing squarely on the state of our house.

I want you to think about what you might need to happen to stay. Write a list. Anything and everything you would possibly want to change about this house. Those were Nick's words—frustrating as they are. I hadn't had time to process his request before Zoey called me over, dropping her bombshell on me like a ton of bricks. I'm surprised I even remembered the conversation.

The house...where to even begin? Everything needs attention. I could compile Nick's precious list, come up with a renovation plan so extensive it would make his head spin, but it wouldn't change the fact that we've outgrown our house.

What I don't understand is why he's so against moving somewhere new. Memories aside, the house I showed him wasn't grandiose by any means, but it was laid out in a much more functional way. We'd all have our own rooms, I'd have a den to use as an office, and we'd have more space for storage.

It's a win-win, and if Nick can't see it, I'll just have to convince him. I'm the one who spends the most time at home —working, taking care of the kids, managing the household. It seems only logical that my opinion on whether to move or stay would carry more weight. The fact Nick might think otherwise makes my frustration simmer just below the surface.

Honk!

I snap back to reality, realizing I've been daydreaming too long and am holding up the carpool line. I release the brake and surge forward to close the gap between me and the car in front of me. From the passenger seat, Stella giggles.

"I was calling your name for a while there, Mrs. Dawson."

"Stella, you can call me Colette, you know that," I say with a smile, though my thoughts are still tangled in the mess of my life.

Finally, we reach the drop-off point and the kids scramble out of the car. "Just assume I'll be picking you all up again this afternoon," I call after them. I watch them disappear through the school doors, unsure if any of them have heard me.

Honk!

I release a slow breath, resisting the urge to roll my eyes or wave my hand in the air. Instead, I press my foot on the accelerator and pull away from the school, heading back home.

The drive back is a blur. My mind is still occupied with the tangled web of my thoughts—Zoey's crumbling marriage, my own unresolved issues with Nick, the state of our house, and the growing realization something has to change before everything falls apart.

If I'm being honest with myself, the housing issue is distracting me from the bigger problem—my marriage. I've become so adept at pretending everything is fine amid the chaos of my life that I've extended the pretense to my relationship with Nick. But now, with Zoey's crisis forcing me to confront the fragility of even the strongest marriages, I know it's time to face the truth. We can't keep going like this, stuck in a cycle of exhaustion, stagnation, and predictability. It's time to see if Nick and I can find our way back to resembling something close to what we used to be.

There has to be a way out of the chaos, a way to reclaim the connection we once had, without blowing up our lives—or our children's. It won't be easy, but I'm determined to try.

As I pull into the driveway and turn off the car, I make a decision. I'll take Nick's challenge to heart. I'll make a list—everything and anything we need to change about our house. But more importantly, I'll start another list, one to address the things we need to change in our marriage. It's time to stop pretending and start fighting for what matters most.

Because if I don't, I know exactly where we're headed—and I'm not willing to let that happen.

With a deep breath, I get out of the car and head inside, ready to face whatever comes next.

CHAPTER
SIX

The daze that settles over me during the drive home from school drop-off lingers throughout the day, weaving in and out of my thoughts as I try to focus on work. But no matter how hard I try, my mind keeps wandering back to thoughts of marriage—both Zoey's and my own. It's hard to believe she hasn't demanded more answers from Aaron, pressed him for every sordid detail. If I were in her shoes, I would drive myself mad, piecing together the fragments of information, conjuring up the most improbable scenarios involving Nick and another woman. But Zoey seems oddly immune to these thoughts, or perhaps she's just numb, her emotions dulled by the shock of it all. Maybe that will change with time, as the reality of her situation sinks in.

As the days go on, and I spend more and more time with her, I begin to sense she isn't telling me everything. Granted, she has every right to share only what she's comfortable with, but I can't shake the feeling there's an important piece of the puzzle missing.

When I share this concern with Nick, he seems genuinely

surprised. We're in bed at the same time for the first time in what feels like months.

"I thought you gals told each other everything," he says, turning to face me.

I smile sadly. "I thought so too, but I had no idea their marriage was anything less than perfect until a week ago."

"What do you think she's withholding?" he asks, his brow furrowing in concern.

"I don't know," I admit, feeling a bit foolish. "Maybe I'm imagining it. But it almost feels like there's another side to the story she's afraid to tell me. I didn't think it could get worse than her suspecting something was going on and doing nothing about it."

Truthfully, there's a small part of me that imagines this whole thing as an elaborate prank. As if, unless I see Aaron and hear the confession come from his own mouth, it couldn't possibly be true. But the next morning, I know how silly I'm being. Of course, it's real. Of course, it's happening. I'm witnessing firsthand the potential end of my best friend's marriage. And I feel completely helpless. No amount of homemade dinners I take over, carpools I manage, or tight hugs seem to make a difference.

And then there's the issue of my own marriage, which desperately needs its own kind of resuscitation. I feel just as helpless when it comes to figuring out what to do.

The obvious first step would be to sit down with Nick and start a conversation, but these days, that seems about as likely as Zoey suddenly wanting to know all the sordid details of her husband's affair. The truly sad part, the part hard for me to wrap my head around, is Nick and I used to have the most incredible conversations. Nothing was off the table—and I mean nothing. How has it become so difficult, in just fourteen years, to even think about uttering the words, *we need to talk about our marriage?* Shouldn't time have made us better communicators? And why has he never said anything to me? Surely, he can't think any more highly of our status quo than I do.

Once again, I'm picking up the slack. No wonder I'm so tired.

————

A string of obscenities flies from my mouth before I have a chance to temper my feelings. The pain from stepping on a cluster of LEGO pieces wedged into the bottom of my right foot is searing, sharp, and completely unexpected.

Life: 3, Colette: 0.

"Benjamin Nicholas Dawson, get your butt down here right now!" I yell, my voice echoing through the house. Like every child in the history of the world who has ever been called by their full legal name, Ben knows to come running.

He skids to a stop a few feet from me, his face pale with worry. "Yeah, Mommy?"

I make a show of lifting my foot, revealing the marks the LEGO pieces have left behind. Out of the corner of my eye, I see Nick enter the room, hesitating in the doorway. "I need you to be better about putting your stuff away. We all have to work a little harder at cleaning up after ourselves, okay?"

Ben nods, his eyes wide, but remains frozen in place.

I exhale softly, my frustration ebbing. "Now please, Ben."

As he hurries to clean up, I pass Nick on my way to the kitchen, and he follows me. "I told you we need more storage, Nick. I can't keep living like this." I fill the kettle with water and drop an Earl Grey tea bag into my second favorite mug, the one stamped with MAMA BEAR. The caffeine might keep me up, but I figure the comfort of tea is more important than a few hours of sleep.

"Maybe the problem is that we have too much stuff," Nick says, his voice even.

I could *growl* like the bear on my mug, I'm so mad. Or scream until Nick, assuming I've gone mad, simply gathers the kids and walks out the door, never to return. Instead, I lift my gaze from the kettle to the cabinets in front of me. I close my eyes, imagining myself in a lush, endless green field with the most beautiful blue sky above. I do everything I can to channel a sense of calm. Then, slowly, I turn to face my husband.

"We could get rid of every single toy, every book, or stuffed animal, or completely unnecessary item in this house, and we still wouldn't have enough room." I speak calmly, evenly. "So I don't want to hear you say that ever again."

Nick stares at me, his eyes wide, clearly contemplating his next words very carefully. Finally, he says, with a forced calm, "It probably couldn't hurt to go through things and see if there's anything we can get rid of. Studies have shown that adults and kids who live in disorganized homes are more likely to experience behavioral problems. And it contributes to higher family conflict."

"Are you kidding me right now?" I shoot back, my voice tight with disbelief. "I was the one who told you about the study, Nick, because we're drowning in this house like I've been telling you for months." I turn my back to him to pour the water for my tea. "And I notice you didn't quote the part of the study that found the levels of the stress hormone cortisol were higher in mothers whose home environment was cluttered."

"I know it's affecting you, I—"

"Then help me do something about it instead of saying I'm the problem."

He scoffs. "I never said you're the problem."

"Maybe not, but you're essentially dismissing everything I say."

"I told you I could fix it, Letty. I told you to make a list of what you want done and I can make it happen. Have you given any thought to that?"

I turn back to him, sipping my tea a little too briskly and burning my tongue as a result. "Sure I've given it some thought—about as much thought as you gave the idea of moving into one of those houses I showed you."

A feeling not too unlike pride swells in my chest, knowing I've shut him up.

I continue, emboldened. "And who do you think is going to be the one to sort through everything to determine what to keep or give away, huh? I'll give you a clue: me, me, and oh yeah—me." I start to walk away. "I'm going to catch up on some work. You let me know when you're ready to take my idea seriously, and then maybe I'll consider yours."

But I don't go back to work. I don't even turn on my computer. Instead, I sit on the edge of the bed, stewing in my frustration. When the feelings don't subside after finishing my tea, I stomp over to my desk, yank open the middle drawer and pull out the legal pad Nick gave me last week. I find a pen and hastily scribble RENOVATION LIST across the top. Then I begin.

I try to recall the items I'd thought up the other day:

1. Update kitchen
2. More storage
3. Paint…everything
4. Dedicated office space??
5. Replace flooring

But the further I get, the more annoyed I become. Renovating the house would be far too disruptive. How can Nick not see that? He can be so hard-headed sometimes, so rigid and stubborn. He hasn't always been this way, and I don't know what has brought it out of him.

Frustrated, I flip the pad to a fresh page, suddenly inspired to create a new list.

1. I have to take care of almost everything at home despite both of us working full-time
2. No romance, little sex
3. I don't feel appreciated—when was the last time I heard thank you?
4. He knows little about the day-to-day details of what's going on in the kids' lives
5. He has to be taught basic life skills—loading the dishwasher/laundry
6. He gives me the silent treatment when he's mad
7. He micromanages the budget/makes me feel bad about spending
8. I always have to be the bad guy when it comes to parenting (because I'm home more)

I take the legal pad to the bed to reread what I've written. I add two more items to the list:

9. Doesn't consider my feelings
10. He has a hard time considering things from others' perspectives
11. We've stopped trying to look good for one another

I pause for a moment, sitting with my feelings of annoyance and discomfort—just like my therapist has taught me.

Then, across the top of the page, I write INVENTORY OF MARITAL PROBLEMS in bold letters. Slowly, I walk to the other side of the bed and bury the pad beneath a pile of magazines in the drawer of my nightstand.

Damn, it feels good to get that out of my system.

———

The next night after dinner, I go to check on Zoey. I've purposely made extra macaroni and cheese to take over, but when I arrive, the house is eerily quiet. I call out each of their names in turn. Finally, Stella appears at the top of the stairs.

"She's been in bed all day," she says, her voice small. I wonder for the millionth time what, if anything, Zoey has told the kids. I haven't had the heart to bring it up, and she hasn't volunteered the information.

"Thanks, sweetie. There's dinner in the kitchen if you're hungry."

Stella rushes past me as I head for the master bedroom, which I find shrouded in darkness. I whisper Zoey's name through the black, eventually finding her curled up in the center of the king bed, her breathing shallow. I approach her carefully and brush my hand through her hair, waking her as gently as I can. She stirs and looks up at me with swollen eyes. My heart aches for her.

"Have you eaten anything?" I ask, my voice soft.

"I'm not hungry," she mumbles, turning her face into the pillow.

I hold in a sigh. "I know, but you've got to eat. Can I make you something? What about soup? Soup is easy."

In the end, I feed her half a bowl of soup, spoonful by spoonful, as she sits in bed. She's too weak, too emotionally drained, to resist. When she's done, she asks to be left alone, and I kiss the top of her head before leaving.

I'm halfway down the walkway when I see Aaron step out of his car ahead of me. Even in the dim light, I can see what the past week has done to him—his face is drawn, his eyes hollow, and his posture slumped. It's clear he's in pain, even if he's the one who has caused it. I'm not sure if he's waiting for me, or if our encounter is purely coincidental, but as he approaches, I find myself frozen, unsure of what to do. Over the years of my friendship with Zoey, I've come to care for Aaron as well. The idea of confronting him now, after everything, leaves me conflicted.

But before I can make a decision, Aaron closes the distance between us and pulls me into a hug. It's brief, almost desperate, and when he pulls away, he looks embarrassed.

"How is she?" he asks, his voice strained.

Our eyes meet, and I debate how to respond. "You've really hurt her," I say finally, my voice cold. I turn to walk away, but he follows me—across the street and up the walkway to my front door, where I finally turn and hold up a hand to stop him.

"We've hurt each other," he says softly, his eyes pleading.

I open my front door a crack and look back at him. "I don't have time for this, Aaron. On top of my already hectic life, I now have to take care of my best friend—which I'm happy to do—but right now, I'm exhausted and just need to go to bed."

"She didn't tell you the whole story, did she?"

His words make me freeze. The feeling I had that Zoey was holding something back and not telling me the full truth rushes back in full force.

"What do you mean?" I ask, guilt slowly creeping into my bones. I should have waited for Zoey to tell me when she was ready, but now that Aaron has started, I can't stop myself.

"She had an affair first. Years ago."

I shake my head, my mind refusing to accept it. "No, there's no way that's true. Zoey would never sleep with someone else. She loves you." Loves, loved—I don't know which is true anymore.

Aaron steps closer, his face etched with pain, his eyes glistening with unshed tears. "It didn't go that far," he admits, his voice thick. "It wasn't sexual, but it damn well didn't stop it from hurting us."

CHAPTER
SEVEN

After Aaron leaves, I go straight into the kitchen and pour myself a glass of wine. I don't need it, but I want it anyway. I find Nick in the bedroom, still awake, and as soon as I start to tell him what Aaron has revealed, the tears begin to fall. I'm not even sure what I'm crying about—my best friend keeping secrets from me, my messy marriage, the physical chaos of our house, or something deeper I can't quite pinpoint. All I know is I need to escape, so I run to the bathroom and cry into a towel, the only place I can find peace amid my unraveling emotions.

When I finally calm down and wash my face, I return to bed to find Nick still awake, his eyes full of concern. I climb in next to him with a heavy sigh and try to explain what Aaron has said, but my words feel hollow, like I'm just going through the motions.

"I never would have guessed either of them would be unfaithful," Nick says.

"Me either."

Zoey having an emotional affair makes as little sense to me as Aaron having a physical one. Still, I'm aware both can damage a marriage beyond repair. I don't want their family to fall apart, just as much as I don't want mine to. I want happy endings for all of us.

"I'm sorry, Letty," Nick says softly. "I know you looked up to them as a couple."

His words catch me off guard. Had I ever told him that? It doesn't seem like something I'd openly admit.

"Thanks," I murmur, rolling away from him. I fluff my pillow, the act a feeble attempt to settle my swirling thoughts. "I'm exhausted. I need to get some sleep."

"Colette…" he starts, his voice tinged with hesitation.

"I know…" I whisper. "But I'm too tired right now."

I lie there until Nick's breathing evens out, signaling he's fallen asleep, and then I let the tears flow again.

There was a time when I would have thrown myself into Nick's arms, seeking the kind of comfort only he could provide. But it feels like a lifetime ago. As much as I hate to admit it, something has changed between us—something has been lost, eroded over time, leaving us as mere shadows of what we once were. We have gone from lovers to…whatever this is. Friends? Friends who occasionally sleep together? Friends who occasionally sleep together and happen to have children?

I'm not naive—I know stress plays a huge role in our problems. But what I can't accept is that most of it stems from our home life, a home life Nick could certainly be making easier for me. Yet, no matter how often I ask him to help, he never truly understands what I'm asking for. I'm not asking for help with the children just for one night, nor am I asking him to unload the dishwasher before bed just once. I'm crying for help—consistent help—and he's not hearing a thing.

Sometimes I try to think back to when things started to go wrong, to pinpoint a conversation where we agreed on who would handle what. But there wasn't one. There has never been such a conversation, which means I have simply let it happen. I have let myself take on the lion's share of the household and childcare duties, and now, after months of no intimacy, Nick seems to have stopped even trying.

I can't deny it any longer—Nick and I are facing something far more destructive than the mess in our house, more painful than the secrets my best friend is keeping from me. This isn't just a problem; it's a breaking point, and I don't know if we'll survive it.

I sit up slowly in bed, studying Nick for any signs of movement. When I'm certain he's fast asleep, I reach into my nightstand and retrieve the list I started the night before. I stare down at the last item I added:

11. We've stopped trying to look good for one another.

Without much thought, I add two more items to the list:

12. Passive versus active—always waits for me to tell him what needs to be done (I'm not his mother!)
13. We're not talking like we used to.

Even as I stare at what I feel are some of our biggest marital problems, I know, despite them all, I love Nick. I love that he's a kind father, and how he provides our kids with a clear example of what it means to pursue your dreams and be successful. I love his faithfulness, how he comes home every night, and makes me feel safe in a world that seems to be against women.

To be clear, I'm well are I'm just as responsible for our issues. I've let little annoyances simmer and grow into something much larger, and kept my mouth shut when I should have spoken up. I've played a large part in allowing our sex life to suffer. Certainly I've kept doing things I no longer want to do, and I haven't asked for the kind of help I truly require. I'm just as responsible for the way things have turned out as Nick is.

I talk to Zoey about all those little annoyances. I fantasize with her about the type of man I wish Nick was—the kind of guy who would surprise me with dinner and then throw me down on the bed afterward, somehow managing to clean the dishes in between. I fantasize about him coming home early from work more often, letting his business partner, Will pick up the slack. I fantasize about us having long, meandering conversations like we did when we were first married. Zoey knows about it all, and yet Nick is the one I should be talking to. I can't expect him to change if he doesn't know he's doing anything wrong.

Nick stirs beside me, and I start pushing the pad of paper quickly under the covers. But a moment later, he settles back into sleep. I shake my head, smiling to myself, and then I return the notepad to its spot, hidden deep in the drawer.

As tired as I am, I can't help but think about the last time I remember feeling truly happy in my marriage.

———

It was a Saturday that started like any other. I was up with the kids, who were younger and easier to manage back then, bribed with cartoons and sugar-filled yogurt in squeezable tubes. I had just finished cleaning the kitchen when Nick announced we were going out. Money had been a little tighter back then, with Nick having to inject some of our personal savings into his business to take it to the next level. We had been eating at home almost exclusively, kept the thermostat just a little higher than we'd like, and had even gone so far as to cancel our Netflix and Apple Music subscriptions—which I sorely missed. So when he suggested we go out, I was ready to turn him down until he brought up the idea of going to the farmers' market at Downtown Summerlin, the outdoor shopping center.

I had been asking him to go for months, but he had always had some excuse. I had thought about taking the kids on my own, but I wanted it to be something we all did together.

We were in the car in record time, heading west on Sahara. The kids were covered in sunblock, and armed with hats and water bottles to combat the relentless summer heat. The market was buzzing; no one seemed to be bothered by the desert heat, except my kids who, almost immediately, begged for lemonade from a stand conveniently situated at the market entrance. Nick begrudgingly handed over six-fifty and gave the takeout cup to Anna, who squealed with delight. Ben jumped impatiently next to her as he watched her drink. They were so easy then; my children. Anna, with her glossy brown hair, still wanted to hold my hand, and Ben loved to be carried on Nick's shoulders. They still looked at us as though we could do no wrong.

We spent an hour scanning the stands for deals, picking out the most beautifully plump red strawberries and the biggest eggplant I had ever seen. We studied the hand-painted art and felt the beautiful handmade bracelets between our fingers. In the end, we spent more money than we should have, but after Nick slid his hand into mine on the long trek back to the car, slipping me a lingering kiss when the kids' heads were turned…I forgot about all that.

Nick and I made love that night, right after we put the kids to bed, as though we couldn't possibly wait a single moment longer to be together again.

I would have enjoyed the moment even more if I had known how rare days like it would become.

———

Each time I visit Zoey, it becomes harder not to bring up what Aaron said. But I've decided to let Zoey tell me whenever she's ready—if she ever is. Most of the time, she wants to talk about the kids, reality television—which she's watching a lot of these days—or books, or the state of my marriage. Anytime I try to bring up what's happening with Aaron, she changes the subject. Eventually, I just stop asking.

"Have you decided what you want to do about the house?" Zoey is up and about at least, in the kitchen making coffee when I arrive on Sunday morning. She's showered and dressed, her hair blown out and styled. She looks much more like her usual self.

I sigh. "Doesn't it just seem like so much more work to renovate our place? And who's to say it would solve anything? What if we go through months of renovations and come out on the other end with a nicer-looking but still too-small house?"

"Then you'll get more money for the house when you sell it."

I shrug, not wanting to admit she's right. The bottom line is I don't want to go through a renovation. End of story.

She brings two cups of black coffee into the living room, handing me one. I've already had a cup that morning, and too much caffeine makes me jittery, but I take it and drink it anyway.

"Is this all really about the house?" she asks softly.

I pause, the mug halfway to my lips. "What do you mean?"

"I mean, don't you see the parallels between what's happening with the house and what's happening with you and Nick?"

I stare at her blankly. "I have no idea what you're talking about."

"Far be it from me to say anything at all about marriage

right now, but it seems to me like you're looking for the quick, easy solution when it comes to the house, and—"

"And I'm looking for a quick and easy solution when it comes to my marriage?"

She shrugs, her mouth forming a straight line. "Well, are you?"

I want to be angry, to release a torrent of words in my defense, but Zoey is right. It isn't the first time I've tried to take the easy way out. Despite being a talented soccer player, I refused to try out for the high school varsity team because there was too much competition, and I was afraid I wouldn't make the cut. I got an English degree instead of a business degree, which would have been the smarter move. And now, I'm ready to abandon the house my children have grown up in because I don't want to live through a renovation.

Don't even get me started on what I think I'm achieving by putting together a list of my marital problems I have no intention of sharing with my husband.

Zoey puts her hand on my knee. "I can tell by your silence you know I'm right, and you're thinking about how you can make it better."

"I'm supposed to be the one helping you, Zo." I meet her gaze and hold it. "Are you ready to talk about what's going on? Have you told the kids anything?"

She shakes her head vehemently. "They think he's away for work."

"For two weeks? They're eleven; they're going to catch on that something's wrong—if they haven't already."

"I'll deal with it when I have to," she says. She sounds nothing like her usual self. I've never known her to back down from a challenge, to simply pretend it doesn't exist. But that's exactly what she's doing.

I think again of what Aaron has told me.

"Is there anything you're not telling me? About what happened leading up to the affair?"

Zoey frowns, her eyes narrowing. "What do you mean?"

"Nothing," I say quickly, offering a sad smile. "I guess I'm just trying to understand."

"You and me both."

She sends me on my way not long after, feigning exhaustion. I bring the twins home with me, watching them bound up the stairs excitedly, and find Nick in the kitchen, reading the news on his tablet. I retrieve the renovations list from my nightstand, carefully tearing it away from the rest of the pad and set it down on the table beside him.

I won't be the type of woman who takes the easy way out time and time again.

"Okay," I say, ignoring the knot of unease in my stomach. "Let's do it."

I'm going to have to trust we can make this work.

CHAPTER
EIGHT

I wake up the next morning instantly hit with a wave of regret.

Why did I tell Nick I wanted to go forward with renovations? Is it just because I want to prove to myself I can resist taking the easy way out for once? Because the truth is, I want to move. I want to start fresh in a house I know for a fact will work for us, instead of spending all our time and money on something not guaranteed to solve our problems.

But admitting this to Nick? Never. I've agreed to the renovations, and I'm going to follow through with my end of the bargain. But no one said I have to enjoy it. I can, and will, seethe in private.

The renovations list is still on the table where we left it the night before, except now there's a sticky note stuck to it. Written in Nick's handwriting, it says: *Is this all? Think deeper. The sky's the limit.* If he were around, I'd point out that the sky is *not* the limit—there are zoning restrictions and budgetary constraints, and besides, I have no intention of living in renovation purgatory longer than necessary.

Still, I take his note to heart, and as I go about my day—

carting the kids to school, working, picking them up, and preparing dinner—I give the list some more thought. By the time Nick is home for the night, I've added eleven items. If the sky's the limit, I'm going to dream big.

1. Update master shower
2. Proper shelving for my books
3. New window coverings
4. Replace door hardware
5. Paint exterior
6. Replace banister
7. New sinks in guest bathroom
8. Replace front door
9. New back screen door
10. Update backyard landscaping
11. Organize garage

As I plate the fettuccine Alfredo, I watch from the corner of my eye as Nick notices the additions to the list. His expression gives away nothing.

Over dinner, I attempt to make small talk with Anna and Ben, all the while urging Ben to keep eating. I thought making him one of his favorite meals might mean a night off from begging, but I'm wrong.

"Ben, please." We've been sitting at the table for fifteen minutes, and he's barely touched his pasta. "You need to eat."

Nick finally chimes in. "I saw some cookies in the pantry, bud. If you want dessert, you have to finish your dinner."

I pinch my eyes shut. "Nick," I growl under my breath.

He turns to me, confusion etched on his face. "What?"

Not to play into the whole stereotypical wife thing, but if he doesn't know what he's done wrong, I'm certainly not going to tell him. And I'm not about to argue in front of the kids. So instead of responding, I roll my eyes and shove an overflowing forkful of noodles into my mouth.

When everyone has finally eaten, I begin my least favorite task of cleaning up the kitchen. Nick buzzes around me as I tidy, making himself look just busy enough to avoid helping. I scrub the pot in my hand even harder, channeling my resentment into each swipe.

Eventually, the dishes are done, and I make myself an Earl Grey tea I intend to drink while catching up on *The Bachelorette*. But Nick stops me as I try to brush past him at the table.

"I wanted to thank you," he says. The sincerity in his eyes stops me in my tracks. "I know staying and renovating the house isn't your first choice, so thank you."

I smile, not knowing what to say. I've settled on seething in private, after all.

"This business with Zoey and Aaron...it really makes you think."

Now he has my full attention. I sit down at the table across from him.

"I think maybe we've lost ourselves a little."

My nose twitches. "Okay..."

He reaches out and takes my hand. "They were so great, you know, and if something like this can happen to them, it makes me think maybe we need to check in a little more with each other."

"Yes," I say, because really, what else is there to say? I mean —describing it as needing to check in more with each other isn't exactly thinking big picture, but it's a start.

I wait for Nick to say more as I slowly sip my tea, but he seems lost in his own thoughts, staring at the list in front of him. Finally, after I've finished my drink and rinsed my cup, Nick gets up from the table and turns to me. I don't know what I expect him to say—maybe apologize for not being more present, for not helping more around the house. Instead, he kisses me on the temple and says, "I think I might have someone from work come look at the house this week. It would be good to have someone to run some ideas by, see what's doable and what's not."

What I want to say is: It all needs to be done.

What I actually say is nothing.

————

The doorbell catches me by surprise, but the real surprise is the gorgeous man standing on my front porch when I swing open the door. He looks about my age, with dark wavy hair graying at the temples. To call him "fit" would be an understatement. Naturally, I've chosen this particular morning to skip my usual shower, so my hair is piled high on my head in the messiest of buns, and my dark under-eye circles are on full display. The only silver lining is I have at least brushed my teeth.

"Can I help you?" I ask, mustering the sweetest voice I can.

"Mrs. Dawson, I'm Zac. I work with Nick. He asked me to come take a quick look at the house. Is now a good time?"

Nick has sent this hunk of a man over without warning me? I'm going to kill him in his sleep.

"Call me Colette." I step aside. "Come on in." I look down at my shabby clothing. "I just finished working out, so you caught me at just the right time."

It's the perfect lie to explain my appearance.

Life: 3, Colette: 1.

Zac follows me into the kitchen, where he sets down his keys, wallet, and phone on the table. "So, Nick told me a little bit about what you guys were thinking in terms of renovations, but walk me through it again, if you don't mind." His voice is—not to sound like a cliché—gravelly and confident. Masculine in every sense of the word.

I show him around the space, growing more and more embarrassed by the state of things as time goes on. "As you can see, we're in desperate need of more storage. And I work from home, so I need some sort of dedicated office space. At this point, I'd settle for anything as long as it fits my desk and chair. Those two things are the most important to me."

He produces a notepad from his back pocket and scribbles something down. "And what else are you thinking in terms of upgrades?"

I release a deep breath. "The house was originally built in 2001, and we haven't really done much to change it. The kitchen and master bathroom are both pretty outdated. I'd like to replace most of the carpet and flooring, some of the older hardware too. The whole place could use a new coat of paint, plus the front door and screen door need to be replaced. I'd really like some real bookshelves so my babies aren't scattered around the house, gathering dust." I feel my cheeks flush. Babies? "I'd love to have the exterior of the house painted and fix up the landscaping, but I don't think that's your concern. Oh—and the banister. I hate it. It's got to go."

Zac chuckles. "So, more storage, a dedicated office space, bookshelves, and a general update on pretty much everything else, including the exterior."

I chuckle too, suddenly feeling a little lighter. "Nick did say the sky's the limit."

"You certainly took his words to heart," he says, and then he winks—a real, non-ironic wink. It's so sincere that I'm able to resist the urge to tease him the way I desperately want to.

We've circled the house and are back in the kitchen, near his things resting on the table as though he has set them there after coming home from a long, hard day. I look at them and back up at him, feeling suddenly shy.

"Well, I certainly have some ideas after seeing the place," he says. Then he leans forward as if about to share a secret. "But those new houses up Charleston really are pretty great."

I blush like a seventh grader getting her first kiss. "You've seen them?"

He shrugs, smiling. "I like to check out all the new housing developments. I would call it professional research, but really, it's just plain curiosity."

I practically collapse into one of the chairs, exasperated. "So you can see the appeal! The house is perfect. We wouldn't have to do a thing. We just pack up—which he knows I'll handle anyway—and move. No renovations, no living in dust and debris, no trying to stop making sense of the senseless. But no, Nick's made up his mind, and what he says goes. It doesn't matter what I want. It doesn't matter that—"

By some miracle of self-restraint, I manage to stop myself from saying more. But the damage is done. I've opened my mouth and unleashed a verbal tirade on someone I've just met. Someone who, up until this moment, I've been trying to impress for some reason or another. My husband's employee to be exact. I'm so far beyond the line of acceptability that I just want to crawl into a hole and disappear.

Mercifully, Zac laughs, though I can tell he's uncomfortable. Then he gathers his things from the table and heads toward the door, turning back to look at me one last time.

"I'll let you deal with all that. And you tell Nick to let me know what you decide. It was nice to meet you, Colette."

All I can muster is a lame-sounding, "Same." And then I close the door behind him, pressing my back against the solid wood and sliding down until I'm sitting on the floor. Only when I'm certain Zac is long gone do I scream, letting out all the frustration built up inside me.

After four more days of trying and failing to get Zoey to open up to me about the state of her marriage, I'm exhausted. This is the same woman who has asked me to look "down there" when she thought she felt something funny. The same woman who has told me about the threesome she and Aaron almost had before they were married. The same woman who has admitted to sleeping with one of her married college professors. I can't understand why she refuses to talk to me about this.

And so I do something I've told myself I wouldn't do.

"I ran into Aaron a while back," I say slowly. "He told me something I'm not sure you wanted me to know."

Zoey's face pales. "What did he say?"

I should stop there. I should stick with my plan to wait until she feels comfortable telling me herself. "He said you had an emotional affair first."

Her response is oddly calm. "Did he now?"

"That's— Did you?"

Her eyes narrow, her tone sharp. "I don't owe you any kind of explanation, Letty. So if you insist on coming over here day after day trying to get me to spill my guts to you, save your breath."

My mouth hangs open as I try to find words. "I don't—what is happening right now? I've been over here every day trying to comfort you, feed you, help take care of your kids. I'm not trying to get you to spill your guts. I just think you need to talk to someone—"

"Maybe I am talking to someone. Did you ever think about that? And as for helping, consider yourself off the hook. I can take it from here."

I blanch. "Zo—"

Her whole body seems to sigh, deflating with exhaustion.

"Just go. Please. I'm tired. I need a break from whatever this is."

"From…You need a break from us?"

"Yes, exactly." Her head bobs up and down almost comically.

"Zo—" I try again, but she cuts me off.

"Please go."

And so I do.

CHAPTER
NINE

At first, I mistake the banging for the beginning of a migraine. But no, I'm not that lucky. The noise is coming from downstairs, where Zac and his small crew are busy demolishing my kitchen, taking it down to its studs. Both Zac and Nick had warned me this would be the worst part of renovating—the loudest, the dustiest, the most disruptive.

Well, count me officially disrupted.

I slam my laptop shut harder than necessary, disconnect it from the charger, and gather the rest of my things. I head downstairs, feeling the tremors from the machines on the floor beneath my feet. A long sheet of thick plastic separates the stairs from the main floor, and I push through it cautiously, like stepping through a veil into another world.

On the other side, I'm greeted by the sight of controlled chaos. The guys are tearing cabinets off the walls, their arms moving with practiced brutality. The beige tile flooring I once hated is gone, the kitchen island is gone—everything is gone, except for the dust clinging to every surface. The space feels gutted, unrecognizable, like a skeleton of what it once was.

I feel absurdly out of place in my own home. I wait for a

lull in the noise before I wave my arms, hoping to catch Zac's attention. After a moment, he notices and makes his way over, boots crunching on the debris-strewn floor.

"I'm going to find a coffee shop to work in," I shout over the noise, hugging my laptop to my chest like it might protect me from the chaos. My eyes sweep over what used to be my kitchen again, taking in the mess I can't seem to mentally process.

Zac offers me a sympathetic shrug, wiping his dust-covered face with his sleeve. "Yeah, sorry about all this. Like I said though, this is the worst part. It'll get better from here."

I nod, but I don't feel reassured. "You've got my number if you need anything," I say, taking a step back toward the stairs, the plastic sheet already swaying in the draft from the open front door.

"Good luck finding some peace and quiet," Zac calls after me, his voice barely audible over the racket.

But peace is elusive.

At the coffee shop, I find a new kind of noise, just as relentless as the demolition at home. The usual quiet is interrupted by the loud, hyper chatter of a group of mothers and their toddlers, and the baristas are buzzing around behind the counter, moving with such exaggerated energy I wonder if they've had too many shots of espresso. Their constant, rapid-fire conversations add to the noise, making it impossible to concentrate.

I give it a solid twenty minutes, trying to drown out the sound with my headphones, but it's hopeless. The din around me claws at my focus, and I can't seem to block it out. Frustrated, I give up and start browsing the Barnes & Noble fiction bestsellers list, adding books to my cart as a form of retail therapy. It's a weak escape, but for a few minutes, it feels like I'm in control of something, even if it's just my online shopping habits.

But my mind keeps wandering back to the mess at home. The sound of walls coming down, the dust that seems to settle on everything, and the discomfort of having strangers rip apart the place where I used to cook dinner, where the kids did their homework at the counter, where Nick and I shared our quiet, stolen moments. Now it's just debris and noise. And Zoey. Always Zoey. Two weeks since she kicked me out of her house—two agonizing weeks where I've had to stop myself from walking across the street, knocking on her door, and demanding to know what's going on. I tell myself she's just going through something. She'll come around eventually. Won't she?

I catch myself zoning out, staring blankly at the group of girls next to me. Their laughter brings me back to reality, and I realize I've been watching them without realizing it. I mutter an apology and turn back to my screen. That's when I notice Zoey's name in my inbox.

My heart skips a beat. The subject line is simple:

I'm sorry.

I hesitate, my fingers hovering over the trackpad before I click it open. My heart thuds in my chest as I scan the short message.

Colette,

I know you've been trying to help, and I appreciate it. But I just need space right now. I'm sorry for how I spoke to you. I just… I can't deal with everything at once, and I need time to figure out what's happening with Aaron and me. Please understand I need time. We'll talk soon.

Zoey

Her words feel like both a lifeline and a sucker punch. I've been so desperate for any kind of communication from her that even this tiny message is a relief. But the words "I need time" ring hollow. Time is the last thing I want to give her.

I try to refocus on my work, but I can't shake the heaviness of Zoey's email. What isn't she telling me? I feel shut out, helpless, like there's a wall between us I don't know how to break down. By the time I pick up Anna and Ben from school, my mood has soured, the stress from home and Zoey's rejection simmering under the surface.

"Why do we have to live in a construction zone?" Anna gripes the moment she climbs into the car. "It's so embarrassing! I told Lily I'd invite her over, but our kitchen looks like a bomb went off!"

"Anna, I've explained this a hundred times. It's temporary. The renovations will be worth it when they're done," I say, trying to keep my voice steady.

"It's taking forever! And I'm sick of eating takeout! Why didn't we just move like you wanted?" she huffs, crossing her arms and staring out the window.

Her words sting, but I bite back a retort. "We'll have a new kitchen soon. Just be patient."

Her silence is loud, and Ben stays quiet in the back seat, clearly picking up on the tension. The drive home feels long, and when we finally walk through the door, the noise from the kitchen crashes into us like a physical wall.

"Great," Anna mutters sarcastically before stomping up the stairs to her room.

I watch her go, a wave of exhaustion washing over me. The house is a disaster, my best friend isn't speaking to me, and now even my daughter seems to be slipping away. I want to scream, to let it all out, but I can't. I have to hold it together for Anna, for Ben, for Nick. For everyone.

Later, I sit alone in the living room with a glass of wine,

and the noise finally subsides. Zac and his crew are gone, leaving behind a gutted kitchen and a layer of dust that feels like it's seeped into my soul. I miss Zoey. I miss the way she'd just show up unannounced, her easy smile, the way she'd listen without judgment. Without her, I feel untethered, like I'm floating through my days without an anchor.

The house feels empty, even though Nick and the kids are upstairs. I feel empty.

I stare at my phone, wondering if I should text her, but what would I say? I miss you? I need you? The words feel too vulnerable, too raw. Instead, I set the phone down and let the silence wrap around me. Everything feels like it's crumbling—my home, my friendships, my family.

I blink back the tears threatening all day. It's not just the house. It's everything—losing Zoey, the chaos at home, the tension with Anna, and the growing distance with Nick. The fear gnaws at me, whispering even when the renovations are done, the house still won't feel like home.

Because how could it, when everything inside me feels so broken?

Finally, I let the tears come. Quiet, desperate tears I've been holding back for too long.

When I've cried enough, I wipe my face and stand. There's no time to fall apart. Not when Anna's upstairs, sulking, Ben needs help with his homework, and Nick's probably working late again.

But as I move through the house, trying to ignore the mess around me, I can't shake the feeling something has to change.

I just don't know how to fix it.

CHAPTER
TEN

I have to learn to work through the noise, to navigate around the messiest areas of the house, and, more importantly, to avoid Zac.

Zac, with his easy charm and those maddeningly good looks making my stomach flip-flop in a way I haven't experienced since Nick and I first started dating. I tell myself it's harmless, just a fleeting attraction. Still, I make sure I look presentable most days—in direct opposition to the frazzled version of myself he encountered the first day—just in case I run into him.

The exhaustion that settled in before the renovations began only deepens as the house becomes harder and harder to live in. We take to wearing shoes everywhere, using and washing a single plate, fork, spoon, bowl, and cup for each of us, and making coffee in the bathroom with the last available piece of counter space. My once-cozy home now feels like a battlefield, each day bringing new challenges and discomforts.

By Wednesday, the kitchen is empty—a blank, dusty slate I can't begin to envision looking any different. Nick, who lives and breathes this kind of stuff, can see the forest through the trees. He seems to relish the process, his enthusiasm a stark contrast to my growing dread. If not for him, I might have thrown in the towel and bought the new house myself. But I try to adopt his excitement, pushing away the nagging discomfort, the ever-present feeling of discontent.

Anna, who has increasingly withdrawn to her room to avoid the growing mess, seems to emerge only when absolutely necessary. Ben, on the other hand, treats the chaos as an adventure. Each day after school, he dashes into the house, eager to see what has changed. His excitement is a small comfort, a reminder that not everyone is as unsettled by the upheaval as I am.

On Thursday, a new crew arrives to lay down the flooring. With them come even more limitations on where we can move in the house. It's about this time I fully regret agreeing to the renovations. The noise, the dust, the constant presence of strangers—it's all too much. I need an escape.

I flee to the library on Friday, desperate for the peace and quiet which is now a distant memory. The serene environment is a balm to my frazzled nerves, a rare moment of tranquility. But even as I work, a sense of unease gnaws at me, a persistent worry something is slipping through my fingers.

When I return home with the kids that evening—after a detour to the bookstore and an ice cream parlor to delay our return—the new wood laminate floor is finally complete. The house, though still chaotic, is beginning to take shape. Nick is already home, an unusual occurrence signaling the importance of the day's progress. He and Zac are in the kitchen discussing the next steps.

Nick's face lights up when he sees us, and he makes a show of kissing each of the kids on the head before giving me a kiss resembling a formality more than a genuine gesture. I catch Zac's eyes lingering on us for a moment before he looks away, the flicker of something unspoken passing between us.

"The floor is beautiful," I offer, trying to sound as enthusiastic as I know Nick wants me to be. I'm dressed in my usual outfit: jeans, a T-shirt, and sneakers. My hair, freshly washed and styled, cascades down my back.

Zac's eyes flick to mine, and I feel a flush creep up my neck. I'm not sure why I care what he thinks, but I do.

"Mom, what's for dinner?" Anna's voice cuts through the moment, dripping with the kind of attitude only a teenager can muster. She may as well be filing her nails absently the way she's projecting her boredom and irritation. Zac looks down at his feet, a smile tugging at his lips.

I glance at Nick, hoping he'll step in, but he just stares back at me, oblivious to the tension simmering beneath the surface. I'm so tired—bone tired—from a long workday still not over, from occupying the kids after school, from pretending everything is fine when it's far from it. I can feel tears threatening to spill, but I hold them back. If Zac weren't standing there, I might let them fall. I might show Nick just how exhausted and fed up I am, and let the kids see their mother has limits too.

"Well, I'll get going," Zac says, breaking the silence. He gathers his things, and Nick follows him to the door. They exchange a few words before Zac finally leaves, the door closing with a soft click behind him.

I stand very still in what will soon be our kitchen once more, waiting to see what will happen next. The kids, perhaps sensing the shift in mood, scamper off, leaving me alone with Nick.

Nick murmurs something under his breath as he crosses the room to inspect where the new flooring meets the wall. The sight of him, so engrossed in the minutiae of the renovation, fills me with a sudden, overwhelming anger. Here I am, struggling to keep everything together, and all he seems to care about is the damn floor.

"Letty? Did you hear me?" His voice breaks through my thoughts.

I force a smile, remembering something I read about how smiling can trick your brain into releasing endorphins. "Sorry, no," I say, trying to inject some lightness into my tone.

"I asked what we're doing for dinner."

The smile slips from my face, replaced by a surge of pure, unadulterated rage.

———

Once I'm sure Nick hasn't followed me upstairs, I go straight for the list I've tucked in the bottom of my bedside table.

- I have to take care of almost everything at home—check.
- I don't feel appreciated—check.
- Doesn't consider my feelings—check.
- Passive versus active—check.

And all within the last ten minutes.

Isn't this the same man who, just a couple of weeks ago, told me he thought we'd lost ourselves? That we needed to check in more with each other? Where is the concern now, when our daily existence is even more complicated, when we are literally surrounded by mess?

I don't have time for this. I didn't have time years ago when I began feeling this way, and I certainly don't have time for it now. Something needs to change—and fast, because the little voice in the back of my head, the one screaming *stop pretending*, is getting louder and more insistent.

I look down at the list. What would happen if I showed it to him? What if I just set it on the table in front of him while he drinks his morning coffee like I did with the renovations list? It is, after all, still a renovations list—just a little more personal, but just as messy. If I show him the list, it might force the communication floodgates open. Sure, it might be difficult at first, but it could be the thing to finally help us fix what has been broken in our marriage.

But who am I kidding? I can't hand over the list. It would be too cruel, and while I have my faults, cruelty isn't one of them.

Just because I can't show him the list doesn't mean there aren't other ways to get my message across. I could, you know, be an adult and use my words.

It's such a compelling idea I almost march myself back downstairs to get started, but my feet feel like they're glued to the floor. It's as though my body knows something my mind doesn't yet understand.

Just then, Ben appears in the doorway, startling me. But once I realize it isn't Nick asking about dinner again, I relax.

"Mommy?"

My sweet, sweet boy. My angel. I've done so much right when it comes to him. Maybe it's because parents are notoriously more relaxed with their second kid, or maybe it's because he reminds me so much of myself—a little on the quiet side, emotional, sensitive.

"What is it, sweetie?"

"I'm hungry."

I smile, feeling the tension in my body begin to melt away. "I know, buddy. I am too. What do you say we go downstairs and see what we can wrangle?"

And just like that, my bad mood is turned on its head.

But as I follow Ben back downstairs, the list still in my hand, I can't shake the feeling I'm on the edge of something— something that, once crossed, there will be no going back from.

CHAPTER
ELEVEN

The text comes in early the next morning, just as I settle into my second cup of coffee. It's from Zoey. My heart leaps as I read her message.

> Thanks for giving me some space. You
> have time to chat later today?

Relief washes over me, and I quickly reply, telling her I'll be over as soon as possible. The weight of the past two weeks —of wondering, worrying, and waiting—seems to lift just a little. Zoey is ready, and whatever she needs, I'll be there.

I pick up McDonald's for dinner—something I desperately try to avoid doing too often—and invite Stella and Sam to share in the feast. Once the kids are set up in Anna's bedroom, giggling over Happy Meals, I leave Nick home to keep an eye on them while I head over to Zoey's.

She greets me at the door with a meek smile, her eyes tired but more focused than they've been in weeks. I respond by pulling her into a tight hug, holding on a little longer than usual, relieved just to have my friend back. Then, with a small flourish, I produce the bottle of wine I've snuck over, raising it like a peace offering.

Zoey's smile grows a little wider as she takes the bottle from me. "You know me too well," she says softly, leading me into the kitchen.

I wait until she's poured us each a glass and we're seated at the kitchen table, the familiar surroundings providing a small comfort. "So, how are you feeling?" I ask, my voice gentle but eager. I want to know everything, but I know better than to push.

Zoey takes a deep breath and downs half her glass of wine in one gulp. "I'm a mess, Letty. I don't know what I'm doing."

I reach across the table, placing my hand over hers. "Anyone would feel the same in your situation, Zoey. You're going through something incredibly hard."

She shakes her head, brushing off my words. "You were right when you said I needed to talk to someone. I don't know why I thought I could figure this out on my own. I guess I was just…ashamed."

"There's nothing to be ashamed of. I'm here for you, whether you want to talk or just sit in silence. Whatever you need."

She blinks slowly. "I loved the way you saw Aaron and me. I could almost make myself believe we were still those people." Zoey looks down at her glass, turning it slowly in her hands. "What Aaron said was true," she begins, her voice barely above a whisper. "I did have an emotional affair." She drains the rest of her wine and sets the glass down with a trembling hand. "It's probably why he was so open to seeing someone else."

"That's not an excuse," I say softly but firmly.

"I know it's not," she replies, her voice thick with emotion.

A thousand questions buzz in my mind—why, when, who

—but I keep them to myself. This is Zoey's story to tell at her own pace.

"I was so lonely, Letty," she continues, her voice cracking slightly. "Aaron was away all the time, and I was stuck at home with the kids, who clung to me every second. You remember what it's like to have only the smallest pockets of time to yourself. The twins were in school, but I was drowning in volunteer work, trying to fill the void of not having a job. I started going to this little Thai place over on Lake Mead and Rampart. They had this incredible tempura spinach salad, and I always seemed to get the same waiter. He was…different. Bright, vibrant, passionate, and handsome—oh, so handsome. I kept telling myself it was the food that kept me going back, but it was him."

I nod, my heart aching for her. "When was this?" I ask gently.

"About four years ago, I think," she says, her voice wavering with uncertainty.

"What happened?" I ask, trying to keep my voice steady.

"It's all such a blur now," Zoey says, shaking her head as if trying to clear the fog. "Somehow, we exchanged numbers, and we started texting about anything and everything. He listened—really listened—like Aaron used to, back when things were good."

I feel a pang of recognition.

"I fell in love with him, Letty," she admits, tears welling up in her eyes. "I'm married, with children, and I let myself fall in love with someone who wasn't my husband."

I push my wine glass aside and reach across the table to take her hand again. "But you stopped. You didn't let it go any further."

She pulls her hand away, her expression hardening. "So what? It's not like I'm better than Aaron just because I didn't sleep with him."

"I know. That's not what I said." My voice is firm but calm. "But yeah, I think it does make a difference. He was sleeping with someone else for two years, Zoey. There's a whole lot of distance between what you did and what he did."

"An affair is an affair," she says, her voice flat.

I shrug, trying to find the right words. "I still think there's a difference. You didn't break your vows, Zoey."

Zoey stands up abruptly and refills her glass, the tension in the room thickening. "Have you talked to him since that first night?" I ask though I'm pretty sure I know the answer.

"No," she says, her voice hollow. "He's tried, of course. But I just…I haven't been in the right frame of mind to talk to him or anyone about it."

I hesitate, not wanting to push her, but knowing I need to say it. "Maybe the two of you need to talk. I mean, he said he still wants to be with you. Do you still want to be with him?"

Zoey looks down into her glass, her expression a mix of sadness and confusion. "Sometimes I think I do. But then this ball of anger rises in the pit of my stomach, and I think I'll be fine if I never see him again."

I open my mouth to respond, but Zoey cuts me off. "I know. I know the kids make it impossible, but it would be so much easier if it was."

My heart aches for her, and for everything she's going through. I don't want to push her into something she isn't ready for, but I can't ignore the thought circling my mind.

"Let me take the kids this weekend. They can have a sleepover, and you and Aaron can have all the time you need to talk."

Zoey looks at me, her expression torn. "But what about the renovations?"

"We'll make it work," I say, my voice filled with determination. "You need this, Zoey. You need to talk to him, to figure out where you both stand."

She moans softly, rubbing her temples. "I don't know if I'm ready. I don't even really know how I feel."

"I think once you two start talking, it will become clearer," I say, knowing full well it's advice I need to take myself.

"What do you think I should do?" Zoey asks, her voice small, almost childlike.

I pause, considering her question carefully. What would I do if I were in her shoes? Nick and I haven't cheated on each other, but our marriage is far from perfect. Still, I have to believe that if you love someone—really love them—you have to at least try to work it out.

"I think it was you who once told me the grass is greener where you water it," I say softly, watching her reaction.

Zoey smiles faintly, a flicker of hope in her eyes. "If only you'd shared your wisdom with me years ago, my marriage wouldn't be such a mess."

We sit in silence for a moment, the weight of our words settling between us. Finally, Zoey speaks again, her voice steadier than before. "What about you, Letty? What do you want?"

I purse my lips, thinking about Nick, the house, the list hidden in my bedside drawer. "Maybe there's time yet," I say, my voice tinged with uncertainty.

Zoey reaches across the table, her hand covering mine. "You deserve to be happy too, Letty."

I nod, squeezing her hand in return. "We both do."

We spend the rest of the evening talking about everything and nothing, letting the wine and the warmth of our friendship soothe the edges of our pain. It's not a solution, but it's a start.

CHAPTER
TWELVE

In hindsight, hosting the sleepover is a pretty terrible idea. Stella and Anna bunk together in Anna's room, but Ben refuses to share with Sam, who he whispers to me in confidence, "smells funny." Sam ends up taking Ben's room, leaving Ben on a makeshift bed of blankets at the foot of our bed, with Mayer curled up nearby. Ben has always been a restless sleeper, tossing and turning like a windmill in a storm. Every sound, every shuffle, jolts me awake, and by the time morning rolls around, I've scraped together maybe four hours of sleep—if I'm lucky.

Desperate for a jolt of energy, I stumble into the bathroom and brew a pot of coffee, rinsing my mug in the sink before drying it with the towel I used the day before. I sip the hot liquid, hoping the caffeine will work its magic. The kids beg for pancakes, so I pull out the portable griddle from our camping gear in the garage and set to work.

"Mom, the syrup is warm," Anna complains as I set the bottle on the table.

I look at her, waiting for the punchline that never comes. "And?"

"I can't put warm syrup on my pancakes. It's disgusting."

I fight the urge to tell her to call me when she has a real problem and instead shrug. "You'll have to make do."

While the other kids dig into their pancakes with luke-warm syrup, Anna sits at the table, arms crossed, her plate untouched. I'm not in the mood for her games, so I purposefully ignore her. When she realizes she's not getting the reaction she wants, she dramatically folds a pancake twice and shoves the entire thing into her mouth before stomping off. I smile after her, trying to summon a burst of endorphins to get through the day.

All I can do is hope Zoey and Aaron have made good use of their time together and that I'll soon hear some good news to counterbalance all the bad of late.

But when Zoey arrives later to pick up the twins, she looks anything but happy. In fact, she looks downright miserable. I try to catch her eye as she waits for the kids to gather their things from the front hall, but she avoids my gaze, focusing on anything but me.

I figure she'll invite me over later or at least text me to give me an idea of how things have gone, but my phone remains silent. The next day comes and goes with no word from her either.

By Monday, with the workers back in the house, any thoughts of Zoey drift to the back of my mind. The kitchen is finally starting to resemble a kitchen again, with new cabinets and countertops being installed. When I return home from carpool, Zac's truck is the only one left outside, and there he is, caulking around our new single-basin sink. We still have no appliances, but at least, in a few hours, I'll have a functioning sink, which means no more washing dishes in the upstairs bathroom.

"It's looking amazing," I say to Zac once the kids have run

upstairs. I'm referring to the kitchen, but the view of him bent over the counter isn't bad either.

"The worst is over, thankfully—at least where the kitchen's concerned." He finishes with the sink and stands up. "This will need to dry for a few hours, but then you're good to go. Backsplash goes in tomorrow, and appliances should arrive the day after."

I squint at him. "How did you manage to take on this project so quickly?"

"I'm pretty new," he explains. "My schedule's a lot lighter than the other guys."

"You seem like you know what you're doing."

Zac chuckles, a deep sound from the back of his throat. "I'm new to the company, not new to construction." He holds up his hands. "These are the hands of a guy who's been in the business since he was thirteen."

"Thirteen? How is that possible?"

He wipes his hands on the towel slung over his shoulder. "My dad was in the business. He taught me everything I needed to know, starting with how to lay tile."

"Is he retired now?"

Zac looks down, his expression shifting. "He passed a few years back. Cancer."

My shoulders drop. "I'm so sorry."

"Thank you."

The air in the room feels heavier, the lighthearted conversation replaced with something more somber. "Anyway," Zac says, trying to shake off the mood. "Me and the guys will be back at the usual time tomorrow. Have a great night, Mrs. Dawson."

"Colette, please," I correct. And then, before I can stop myself, I blurt out, "Are you married, Zac?"

If he's surprised by my question, he doesn't show it. "Divorced."

"Ah." I never know what to say when someone mentions they're divorced. Sometimes, they seem relieved, even happy to be free. Other times, the pain is still fresh, evident in their eyes.

I can't quite place where Zac falls on the spectrum.

"I don't recommend it," he says finally, a hint of regret in his voice.

"Could I ask—would it be too forward to ask what happened?"

I want to hear there were extenuating circumstances, that they wanted different things, or they married too young. I want to hear one of them did something unforgivable because anything else would feel too close to home.

"I think it was a bunch of small things we let pile up until it was too late."

It's exactly the kind of answer I don't want to hear.

"My best friend might be getting divorced," I confess, not sure why I'm telling him. It's not like he's recruiting members for some divorce club.

"I'm sorry to hear that."

I watch as he gathers his tools and heads to the front door. Just before he leaves, he turns back to me. "For what it's worth, I see and hear a lot working in people's homes." He smiles softly. "There's a lot of love in this house."

I stand and watch him go as his words linger in the air.

That night, and for several nights after, I can't sleep. My mind is consumed with thoughts of marriage, Zac's words echoing in my head. I worry over the list hidden in my nightstand and obsess over what happened—or didn't happen— when Zoey and Aaron had their talk. Zoey is still oddly quiet about it, a fact I'm trying and failing not to take personally. It feels as though I've done something wrong. I thought we had moved past what happened, her annoyance with me for talking to Aaron a thing of the past, but her continued silence suggests otherwise.

Determined not to repeat my previous mistake, I decide to wait. I'll be patient. But it doesn't stop me from thinking about her. I can't shake the feeling I've missed something crucial. How could I have failed to notice what was happening in her marriage when I can't even pinpoint the exact moment things started going wrong in my own? It's not like I doubted her stories about their wild sex life or questioned her time spent out of the house. She hadn't told me they'd stopped talking to each other the way Nick and I have.

It doesn't make sense. As my best friend, Zoey knows all about my struggles—how tired I am of pretending, how disconnected Nick and I have become. During any one of our countless conversations, she could have confided in me about her own troubles. We could have supported each other. Misery loves company, after all. But she said nothing.

And so, this, and so much more keeps me up at night until finally, I give up and get out of bed.

In the newly completed kitchen, I put the kettle on to boil. My mother always said most worries could be solved with a cup of chamomile tea, though she married a man who worshipped the ground she walked on and spent every day of their forty-one-year marriage proving it to her. When he passed almost two years ago, they were just as in love as the day they walked down the aisle.

Chamomile tea isn't going to solve my marital problems. Yet as I sip my tea and scan the list that shall not be named, I feel a surge of determination. It's time to fix my marriage. I just have to start. I just have to—

Footsteps behind me catch me by surprise, and I quickly stuff the list into the pocket of my nightgown as Nick appears in the kitchen.

He rubs his eyes, clearly still half-asleep. "Letty? It's almost four a.m."

"I couldn't sleep." I take another sip of tea, trying to calm my racing thoughts. "My mind won't shut off."

"What's going on?" He pulls out a chair and sits down beside me.

I turn to face him, the determination I felt moments ago fading rapidly. Just say it, I tell myself.

"I can't stop thinking about Zoey and Aaron," I say instead, easing into the conversation.

Nick nods. "It's hard to believe we didn't see anything coming. I never would have guessed either of them would go outside their marriage."

I meet Nick's gaze and, as much as I hate to admit it, wonder. *Are you?*

I've never had a reason to question my husband's loyalty before. He's never hidden his phone when I walked into a room, nor have I smelled another woman's perfume on him or found lipstick on his clothes. I've probably taken for granted that he works in a male-dominated field. But if Aaron can cheat, why can't Nick?

"What you said the other week—about us losing ourselves a little… What did you mean?"

He looks pained, though I suspect it's more from the hour than anything else. He sighs before answering. "I mean—we haven't exactly been in sync lately. I work a lot, and you're so busy with the kids and—"

"I work just as much as you do. You just don't see it."

He rests his hand on my forearm, his touch warm. "I know you do. I'm sorry."

"I don't want to end up like them," I say quietly. "And I think the only way to avoid it is if we're more honest with each other."

He's silent for a moment, then asks, "Is there something you haven't been honest with me about?"

It takes me a few seconds to lift my gaze to meet his eyes. Finally, I find my voice. "I think there's a lot I've kept from you because it was just easier. Or maybe because, if you weren't figuring it out on your own, it meant you weren't paying attention. And then maybe it wasn't my responsibility, but yours."

Nick rubs his eyes again, looking exhausted. "That's a lot to digest at four in the morning."

I get up and rinse my empty cup in the sink. "Try being in my head."

He shakes his head, smiling slightly. "No, thank you."

I stand beside his chair, studying him. He's still so handsome, and he'll probably only get better looking with age, while I feel like my attractiveness is fading by the day.

Nick's voice is soft when he speaks again. "What haven't you been telling me, Letty?"

The moment I've been hoping for, the opening I've yearned for, is finally here. But now I feel suddenly incapable of seizing it. My body has finally caught up with the reality that four a.m. is a ridiculous time to be awake.

I don't say anything for a while, unable to find the right words to explain I started this conversation but now just want to go to bed instead of finishing it.

Nick doesn't press me. Instead, he gets up from the table and takes my hands in his, his grip gentle but firm. "I think maybe it's a tough time to be processing these kinds of emotions," he says. I frown, not understanding, and he continues, "Are you sure you're not letting what's going on with Zoey get to you? Maybe your emotions are a little heightened. Maybe—"

I pull my hands away. "You're kidding, right?"

But I don't wait for an answer.

Upstairs in our bedroom, I pull the crumpled list from my pocket and shove it into the bottom of my nightstand drawer. When I turn to pull back the covers, Nick is standing on the other side of the bed.

"Listen, I'm sorry—"

My shoulders droop. "I'm tired, Nick."

He opens his mouth, then closes it. Eventually, he sighs. "Letty…"

"It's too late for this right now. I need to sleep."

CHAPTER
THIRTEEN

I am so tired I could cry.

When the sun streams through the blinds, my first thought is someone is playing a cruel trick on me—it can't possibly be morning already. My second thought is if I don't get my hands on a pot of coffee immediately, today might be the day I finally resort to murder. On a normal day, I'm useless before my coffee, and today is anything but normal.

I'm in the bathroom, splashing cold water on my face, trying to shake off the exhaustion, when Nick walks in with a cup of coffee. But it isn't the usual quick brew; he's gone all out, using the fancy glass cups so I can see the layers of espresso, milk, and foam, topped with a drizzle of caramel. I take it from him tentatively, like it might bite.

"I was hoping you'd consider this a peace offering," he says.

I study his proposal—fancy coffee in exchange for dismissing my feelings, and telling me I'm letting Zoey's divorce affect me too much. It seems too easy to let him off the hook. I open my mouth, ready to retort, but then close it again, the words escaping me.

Nick looks defeated. "I do think we need to talk more about what you said last night."

"I know," I say quietly. "But we both know now isn't the time. I'm so tired I can barely stand."

"Later then?" he asks, turning to the mirror to rearrange a stray piece of hair. He catches my reflection, waiting.

I want to have this talk, but right now I can't think beyond getting the kids to school so I can crawl back into bed with my laptop, pretending I'll nap between meetings, even though I know I won't. "Sure, later," I agree with a shrug. I know I'm being evasive, maybe even cold, but I can't help it. No one running on this little sleep should be held accountable for their words or actions.

I blame the lack of sleep for what comes next. No one in their right mind would complicate an already tangled situation unless their central nervous system is seriously compromised, and their decision-making skills impaired.

It's no surprise I can't focus on work. Despite consuming enough coffee to power a small village, my brain remains in a fog, unable to form coherent sentences or solve the simplest problems. I can't even sit still for more than twenty minutes before I have to get up and move around.

During one of these restless moments, I find myself downstairs, looking for Zac. There's been talk of redoing the banister or maybe the guest bathroom—either way, Zac is nowhere in sight, though his trusty truck is still parked out front.

I find him in the garage, of all places, erecting a wall. Even if I'd slept twelve solid hours, I'd still be confused.

Zac laughs when he sees my bewildered expression, his hand holding the hammer dropping to his side. "I'm guessing Nick didn't tell you what we had planned?"

I step closer. "Uh, no, he didn't."

"I know it doesn't look like much now, but we can add a

window here for natural light, and of course, we'll insulate properly and install HVAC."

I scratch my head, feeling like a confused monkey. "I'm sorry, you're going to have to help me out here. I'm running on fumes. What exactly are you saying?"

He grins, his smile wide and genuine. "Welcome to your new office."

It takes a moment for his words to sink in, and when they do, I feel the warmth of tears running down my face. Normally, I'd be embarrassed, but I'm too damn exhausted to care. I sink onto the dusty floor and let it all out—the frustrations, the exhaustion, the fears I've been bottling up for who knows how long.

I don't even realize Zac has put his arm around me until the scent of sawdust and something else—maybe men's deodorant—washes over me. He makes a soft, soothing sound that reminds me of how I used to calm Ben when he was a baby. He stays with me until the crying stops, until I lift my head from his shoulder, our eyes meeting. Then I catch myself staring at his lips, my heart pounding in my chest. The thought is there and gone so quickly I can almost convince myself it hasn't happened.

Almost.

Eventually, Zac breaks the silence with a tentative smile. "I can honestly say that was not the reaction I expected." We both dissolve into laughter, lightening the mood.

At some point, we get to our feet, though I'm still feeling unsteady. "Contrary to what just happened, I am grateful. Thrilled, even." I force a smile to drive the point home. "Whose idea was this?"

"It was mine," he admits, a faint blush creeping up his cheeks. "I've done it a few times on other projects."

"It never would have crossed my mind to use the space in

this way." I look around the soon-to-be office, and this time, my smile isn't forced. "Thank you."

His eyes crinkle at the corners when he smiles, the sign of a man who has found happiness in life. "Don't thank me yet. There's still a lot of work ahead."

It feels like a win—finally.

Life: 3. Colette: 2.

———

When I come out of the bathroom, Nick is sitting at the foot of the bed. Once I catch my breath and return to reality, I ask why he's home so early.

"I've got Lucy coming at five-thirty," he says, a smile tugging at his lips. "I'm taking my wife out for dinner. Wherever she wants to go."

He looks so happy, so innocent, so much like the Nick I first met I don't have the heart to tell him I'm still exhausted. The thought of making myself presentable and sitting in a restaurant is about as appealing as a root canal. All I want is to rest, maybe watch an episode of *The Good Witch* with Ben and Anna —the one show that gets both of them to spend time with me.

But instead of saying any of this, I nod. "Sounds like a great idea."

"I'm going to jump into the shower. You think about where you'd like to go."

By the time I hear the water turn on, I've already decided where we'll eat. It isn't a hard choice. Sure, I could've chosen a nice steakhouse on the Strip or Mon Ami Gabi with its view of the Bellagio fountains, or even the Thai place at Red Rock Casino Zoey has been raving about. But there's only one place I want to go.

As Nick showers, I wash my face and apply a small amount

of makeup—just enough to feel like I'm trying. A thin layer of concealer under my eyes, a flick of mascara, a dab of blush applied with my ring finger. My mother's good genes have been kind to me. I pull on a pair of dark jeans and a cream-colored blouse, and slip on the necklace Nick bought me years ago. My hair is a lost cause, so I leave it in the messy waves from my overnight braids.

The doorbell rings right at five-thirty, and I hear Ben rush to greet Lucy with his usual excitement. If I didn't know better, I'd think he had a crush on his babysitter—but he's only eight, forever my baby. I'm not ready for that yet, so I do what any mother in my position would do. I ignore it.

Anna is sprawled on the couch when Nick and I descend the stairs, looking as unimpressed as I expected. At twelve, she's only a year away from being able to stay home alone and hates when we hire a babysitter. But there isn't much I can do to please her these days, so I don't take it personally.

"We'll probably be a few hours," Nick says to Lucy, who, as a freshman at UNLV, looks impossibly young to be in college. Maybe good genes run in her family too.

We're out the door and in the car before Nick finally asks where we're going. I rattle off the address and tell him it's a surprise.

———

Nittaya's Secret Kitchen is exactly what Zoey promised. Small, cozy, and warm. The tempura spinach salad is so good we devour it before our entrées arrive.

Nick is in an unusually good mood considering what we're supposed to be discussing. Meanwhile, my food seems to curdle in my stomach as the minutes tick by. I keep waiting for him to set down his fork, signaling the inevitable shift in conversation, but he seems intent on simply enjoying our night out. It has been a while. I can't even remember the last time we went out, which probably means it has been far too long.

I'm nearly done with my drunken noodles, and Nick with his basil chicken, when it happens. There's no dramatic setting down of utensils, no squaring of shoulders, or even a knowing look. One moment, I'm talking about the kids and the next, Nick leans forward and says my name so simply I know this is it.

"I don't know where to start," I admit. And neither does he.

I stare over his left shoulder, my eyes flitting from one waiter to another, studying them. Any one of them could be him. Any one of them could be the man Zoey fell in love with four years ago.

"Just be honest," Nick says.

My gaze snaps back to his. "About what?"

He sighs, a hint of impatience creeping in. "Are you even paying attention? Because it feels like you're not really here with me."

I swallow hard, trying to push down the lump in my throat. "I'm sorry," I say. But I still don't know where to start. I'm distracted. Coming here was a bad idea.

Nick tries again. "Is there something you haven't been honest with me about?"

Of course, I think of the list. If I knew it wouldn't upset him, I would pull it out and read each item line by line. But I start with the easiest truth.

"I'm exhausted," I say.

"I know you are, and I am too, but we have to talk about this sooner or later."

"No." I shake my head. "I don't mean just today; I mean all the time."

He's quiet for a moment. "I'm not trying to diminish what you're saying, but isn't everyone? I don't think I know any parents with young children who aren't tired all the time."

Not like this, I want to tell him. Other parents are tired from balancing work, caregiving, and life, just like I am. But how many of them are exhausted from pretending? Bone tired from feigning fulfillment and happiness...that they're in a happy marriage. It's all these reasons and more that I'm exhausted.

"I can practically see the cogs in your brain whirring, Letty," Nick says. "Whatever it is, just tell me."

I open my mouth to explain, but what comes out is something completely different. "You never say thank you."

He looks confused. "I—what?"

I try again. "I'm saying I don't feel appreciated—by you or the kids." I could almost forgive the kids for this, but Nick is a grown adult. Surely his mother taught him better.

He swallows, clearly thrown off balance. "What else?"

"I'm tired of having to tell you what needs to be done. If the dishwasher is clean, empty it. If the trash is full, take it out. If we're running low on milk, buy some on your way home from work."

"This is what you've been keeping to yourself? What you're all up in arms over?"

"That!" I snap, pointing a finger at him. "That's how you talk to me."

Nick sits back in his chair, crossing his arms over his chest. I know the move well—it means he's shutting down. Sure enough, a long, pointed silence falls over us.

Eventually, I catch our waiter's attention and signal for the check, which I pay for with cash, leaving a generous tip. Then I get up and walk out to the car. As I fish around in my purse for the keys, I briefly consider driving off without Nick. If he wants to act like a child and give me the silent treatment, I could act like one too.

In the end, I sit in the passenger seat until Nick joins me, starts the car, and reverses out of the parking lot without a word. It's the same old story, just a different day.

"Tell me what I do to upset you," I say.

He glances at me, then returns his eyes to the road. "I'm not doing this now."

"Do you know a better time? Isn't that what tonight's dinner was about?"

He signals and changes lanes. "Tonight was about you being honest with me."

"Look where it's gotten us, Nick. I made two observations, and you gave me the silent treatment, which you always do when you're mad. How am I supposed to have an honest conversation with you if you're going to react like this?"

He says nothing.

"Tell me what I do to upset you," I repeat.

"Fine," he grunts, waiting until he's safely stopped at a red light. "You never initiate sex."

I should have known sex would be his first complaint. Here I am, telling my husband I'm exhausted, I don't feel appreciated, and I don't want to have to tell him to help around the house—and his first concern is my lack of initiating sex. Still, I try to react maturely. Because I'm an adult— and I don't really have a choice in the matter.

"Okay, I hear you," I say. "I'll work on it."

He opens his mouth to speak and closes it again.

"What else?" I prompt.

He hesitates, and I brace myself. "You don't have your own thing," he says finally.

I wait for him to explain. "You don't have any interests or hobbies."

"And you do?" So much for maturity.

He smiles, but it doesn't reach his eyes. "It may be what I do for a living, but I've got construction. You know I love to work with my hands, to stay busy. I worry your entire life is about me and the kids."

"Is that so bad?"

"I mean...maybe it's why you're so exhausted, Letty. You don't have anything that's your own."

Not even ten minutes ago, I was considering driving off without him, and now I'm staring at the steering wheel like it's something I want to rip out of the car. Nothing about this conversation is going according to plan. Every instinct in my body is screaming. *Retreat! Retreat!*

"I think... I think we're going about this all wrong. Maybe we need to look at the bigger picture instead of pointing fingers. Figure out what the real weaknesses are in our marriage." I blink slowly, my exhaustion catching up to me. "When we're better rested."

Even then, I'm not sure I want to hear anymore.

CHAPTER
FOURTEEN

Zac and I have an unspoken agreement: we won't discuss what happened the day he first showed me my new office. Each day, as I spend more and more time talking to him and watching him work during my breaks, it becomes easier to forget it even happened. We talk about how he learned construction while I sip my mid-morning Earl Grey tea, and how I got into publishing while I eat lunch. We delve into the end of his marriage while I pop almonds into my mouth in the middle of the afternoon after the kids have been picked up from school. I find myself saying almost anything just to see those wrinkles at the corners of his eyes, the ones assuring me he's lived a happy life.

I enjoy watching him work, watching my office slowly take shape. So much more goes into a renovation than I'd ever imagined; the repositioning of the water heater, running the electricity, adding a window, insulating the walls. It's a glimpse into a side of Nick's life I've never seen before. And as I watch him work, I start to understand what Nick meant when he said I didn't have something of my own. But what am I supposed to do? I mean—I don't know many thirty-nine-year-olds who just up and adopt a new hobby. I'm too young to take up knitting—okay, that's not entirely true; I just can't stand the sound knitting needles make—I'm terrible at anything resembling a sport, and I definitely don't have the patience for gardening. I love to read, but something tells me it's not exactly what Nick had in mind. It seems like my hobby needs to involve getting me out of the house and away from everyone in it.

Setting my status on Slack to "away," I make two cups of coffee and carry one out to the garage-turned-office.

"I come bearing caffeine," I say as I approach Zac. "But I may have ulterior motives for delivering said caffeine."

Zac greets me with a warm smile. "Okay…"

I take a deep breath. "Do you have any hobbies?"

"Sure," he says, setting down his tape measure and holding the mug with both hands. "I like making pizza."

"I think that's called making dinner."

"Not the way I do it." He flashes his eyes.

"So, what, you prepare your own dough and all that? Really make an event out of it?"

His smile grows. "Exactly."

"Okay," I say, tilting my head. "Anything else?"

He thinks for a moment. "I like putting together playlists."

I frown. "But is that really a hobby?"

"Okay then, tell me what you consider a real hobby."

"Haven't you heard? I don't have any." The words slip out before I can stop them.

He pauses, seeming unsure whether to laugh or frown. He turns over an empty pail, sits on it, and settles his gaze on me. He studies me for a moment. "What about yoga?"

"I'm far from graceful."

"Calligraphy."

"Pass."

"Wine tasting?"

"I taste wine most nights."

He chuckles. "What about learning to read tarot cards?"

"I'm not really into woo-woo stuff."

"Songwriting."

"You do not want to hear me sing."

"Learn about the stock market."

I wince. "Hard pass."

"Take a dance class."

"I'm not graceful, remember?"

"Bird watching."

"I'm too impatient."

"Stamp collecting."

"Okay, now you're just messing with me."

"Parkour."

"Par—what?"

His smile is wide and bright, and hell—it's entirely disarming. I feel the skin on the back of my neck heat up in a not entirely unpleasant sort of way.

"Well, I give up. You're too hard to please."

I think to myself how Nick would probably agree, but I'm too caught up in the fact that, for the first time in as long as I can remember, I'm being flirted with—at least I think that's what this is. And what's more, I'm flirting back. I didn't think I still had it in me.

I'm about to go back for more, like taking another hit of something good, when the image of Aaron stopping me in front of his house flashes in my mind. *She had an affair first. It wasn't sexual, but that didn't stop it from hurting us.*

Chastened, I stand quickly, nearly sloshing coffee from my cup in the process. "Well, I'd better get back to work."

I feel Zac's eyes on my back as I walk away, but I keep going. Upstairs, I splash water on my face and look at myself in the mirror. *Is this how an affair begins? Just like that?*

I don't want to find out.

Affair. It's such an ugly word. It brings out the worst fears in a person. It makes you question yourself, your relationship, maybe even your entire existence. I have no doubt this is what Zoey is struggling with the most. I just wish she would talk to me about it instead of pushing me away. Maybe if she had talked to me four years ago when she started going to Nittaya's Secret Kitchen, everything afterward could have been avoided. I could have talked her out of going back there, and maybe Aaron would never have been open to straying outside of his marriage. Everything could have been so different if she had just spoken up.

But then it hits me. Am I making the same mistakes she did?

It's easy to convince myself I'm not, but the fact remains I've waited far too long to speak up and fight for my marriage.

But I'm going to do so now.

————

The bigger picture is hard to see when all I want to do is point fingers. Especially when I wake up the next morning to find the dishwasher still hasn't been emptied. Nick is at the table with the kids, paying them little attention as he types away on his phone. Just like that, I have another thing to bring up whenever we muster the courage to dive back into the discussion of our marital weaknesses. A week has gone by since our first attempt. Each day, I wait for Nick to bring it up when we're alone, but he doesn't.

Even with my back turned to him, I can feel him watching me. My thoughts are already buzzing with everything I need to do today. After dropping the kids at school, I need to rush back home for an early meeting. After weeks of logistics and driving me crazy in the process, Brent has finally decided it's time to transition a couple of our employees. Emily is going to take over managing the YA imprint from Matt, and Matt will now handle thrillers. It's part of my job to ensure the transition goes smoothly. Today is the first of many steps, and I need to be on my A-game.

The smell of coffee stirs me from my thoughts. Nick made a pot this morning instead of just his usual cup. Noted.

I'm two sips in when Nick approaches me from behind. "I was thinking I could try to bag off early again tonight so we can talk."

I glance at him over my right shoulder. "I've got a busy day today. Could we talk after the kids go to bed?" It's not ideal, but I don't want to push off the conversation any longer.

He nods, a sad smile tugging at his lips. After kissing me chastely on the temple, he does the same to the kids and heads out the front door. Mayer winds around my feet, looking for attention, breakfast, or both.

I turn my attention to Ben and Anna, asking in my best motherly voice, "Who's ready for breakfast?"

After preparing Ben's soft-boiled egg and toast cut into thin strips, and Anna's two blueberry waffles with *cold* syrup, I sit down at the end of the table with my second cup of coffee and a couple of eggs of my own. My mind drifts as I watch the kids hungrily eat. Ben's field trip to Wetlands Park is coming up, and I still haven't filled out his permission slip. Anna will soon need to decide if she wants to play soccer or try something new this season. My gut tells me she might be moving away from soccer toward something more in line with what her small friend group is into at the moment. If only gossiping and staring at their phones built character and taught them teamwork.

As I watch Anna tuck a strand of hair behind her ear, I have the sudden urge to reach out and touch her. To run my fingers through her hair like I used to when she was younger.

It's torture watching my children grow and stop needing me the way they once did. It's almost enough to make me want to keep having babies for as long as I can.

I once felt as though I knew Anna like the back of my hand, but with each passing year, she becomes more of a mystery. She's stopped wanting to share things with me, stopped wanting to spend time with me. She could be sitting right across the table from me, and I would still miss her.

"Anna," I say, waiting for her to look up from whatever video she's watching on her phone. "Why don't you pick a friend to come over this weekend, and I'll take you both to a movie."

She seems to consider my offer. I feel hope balloon in my chest. And then—

"Could you just drop us off so we can go alone?"

I try to hide my disappointment. "Sure, hon."

She graces me with a wide smile. "Thanks, Mom."

"What about you, Ben? Want to see a movie with Mom this weekend?"

Ben looks up at me from his breakfast. "Could Daddy take me?"

I exhale. "I don't know, buddy. You'll have to ask him."

I know what Nick will say. Because, as much as he thinks he hides it well, I've noticed his time spent with the kids is shrinking as the years go on. He's always on his phone, even when he's with them, and he's stopped trying to connect with them, stopped taking an interest in their lives. He was once an incredibly involved father—loving, present in a way I could barely keep up with. But that changed somewhere along the line, and, like so much else, I chose not to speak up.

"You know what?" I reach out and touch Ben's arm. "You pick a movie you'd like to see with Daddy, and I'll make sure he takes you." I turn to Anna. "I'd like you and me to do something together this weekend. Just the two of us. You give it some thought and let me know what you'd like to do."

I practically hold my breath, waiting for a response.

"Okay," she says. "But can I still go see a movie with a friend?"

I nod. It's still a win. And I need all the wins I can get.

CHAPTER
FIFTEEN

The doorbell rings early Saturday morning, rousing the quiet of the house. Ben springs from the couch, always eager to be the first to know what's happening. A chorus of voices follows, and soon Ben appears in the kitchen with Sam and Stella trailing behind him. I'm surprised but happy to see them. Their absence around the house lately had been notable, and I'd assumed it was because Zoey was shutting me out again.

"Hey, guys," I say, glancing at the microwave to check the time. "Have you eaten?"

Sam nods, but Stella looks unsure.

I get up from the table and open the fridge. "I'll whip up some scrambled eggs and bacon in case anyone's still hungry."

They hang around, chatting with each other as I cook. When the food is ready and set on the table, they gravitate toward it, dishing themselves plates and devouring the meal. As I watch Stella, I notice she looks a bit thinner than the last time I saw her. Then again, it could just be that she's getting older, shedding her baby weight—just like Anna. Seeing the two of them together often leaves me feeling rattled by how fast time is passing. They're no longer children but not yet adults, stuck in the in-between stage where everything feels like life or death.

I remember those years vividly—the desperate need to become someone separate from your parents, to carve out a sense of agency. It was a confusing time for me, and I didn't even have to deal with social media.

I drift around the room as the kids eat, tidying up and half-listening to their conversation, the way mothers do. When the food is gone, I start gathering their dishes. As I reach around Sam, I'm hit by a familiar smell—fresh air, salt, and sweat, but underneath it is something else. Something different. He smells…unwashed.

I inhale deeply, just to make sure I'm not imagining things.

Definitely unwashed.

Leaving the kids to their business, I go in search of Nick, finding him standing in front of the sink, a towel wrapped around his waist, his hair slick from the shower.

"Did I hear the doorbell earlier?" he asks.

I nod. "Sam and Stella are here." I hesitate, then add, "Sam kind of smells."

Nick looks at me in the mirror. "What do you mean 'he kind of smells'?"

"I mean, the kid needs a good long scrub under hot water."

"Well," he shrugs, "he's at that age."

I cringe. "This isn't the standard boy smell. He smells dirty, like he hasn't showered in days." I glance toward the door, my mind spinning.

"Don't do it, Letty."

I look back at Nick, chewing on my bottom lip.

"Don't," he says again.

"I just want to make sure she's okay."

His shoulders slump. "She's made it clear she wants space, Letty. You've got to respect her wishes."

"I—"

"You women need to know when to let things go. You harp and nag and push, and all it does is make things worse."

My mouth drops open. "'You women'?"

"Come on, you know what I mean. Guys don't pull this crap. You've got to let it go."

"She's my best friend, Nick. And she's drowning. She might not be able to tell me herself, but I know what's happening."

He turns to face me head-on. "It's a bad idea."

But I'm not listening. I've already made up my mind. I can't be patient anymore.

Fiddling with the house key on my ring, I march across the street. I ring Zoey's bell once, twice, fully expecting her to answer. But I'm left standing there, waiting. She's sent her kids over to my house while she does—what?

I unlock the door, ignoring the anxious feeling twisting in my stomach, and push it open. The first thing I notice is the darkness. Every shade is drawn, every light turned off. Even through the gloom, I can see the place is a mess. Clothes are strewn everywhere, and dishes clutter the counters. I'd bet that if I opened the fridge, it would be nearly empty.

The anxiety in my stomach deepens as I climb the stairs. The kids' bedrooms are remarkably clean, and the bathroom too, but I don't know what to expect as I approach Zoey's bedroom. A part of me hopes to find her asleep, exhausted after the past few weeks, but finally ready to let me in again. I would forgive her silence because it's what friends do.

But her room is empty. And a mess.

I close the door behind me, exasperated. In the kids' bathroom, I find half-full bottles of 2-in-1 shampoo and body wash. There are clean towels and facecloths in the cabinets below the sink. The relief I feel seeing these items is immediate. But now comes the hard part: how do I talk to Sam about the importance of regular showers? It's definitely a conversation that should come from his parents, not me. But I worry one of the kids will say something to him about the way he smells, which would be far more embarrassing than hearing it from me—right?

I think about this as I rinse dishes, load the dishwasher, and wipe down the counters. By the time I've gathered the scattered dirty laundry and started a load of darks, I still have no clue what to do about Sam.

But as I leave Zoey's house, locking the door behind me, I'm buoyed by one simple fact. Zoey will have to come fetch her kids at some point. She'll have to show her face.

———

When Zoey appears at my door that night, just as I expected, I nearly gasp. It's impossible to believe she could look so different after just a few short weeks. Like Stella, she's lost weight, but in Zoey's case, it's all come off her face, leaving her looking gaunt and worn down. Out of habit, I reach for her, my hand encircling her wrist.

I barely choke out her name before she pulls away from my grasp. Looking over my shoulder, she calls out for her kids who, against all odds, come running past me in under a minute. She turns to follow them.

"Zoey," I say, my tone frantic. "What's going on? I thought we were good, and now we're—"

She spins around to face me, her eyes wild. "Stay out of my house. I can clean my own house and do my own laundry. I don't need you babying me."

"I was just trying to help, Zo."

"I don't need it." She shakes her head. "You've got your own family to worry about. I don't need you getting involved in mine."

Nick's words echo in my head. *You women need to know when to let things go. You harp and nag and push, and all it does is make things worse.* But I choose, again, to ignore them.

I follow Zoey down the pathway to the sidewalk. "I don't understand what's happening here. I took your kids for the night so you could talk to Aaron. So you could have some peace and time to figure things out. And something happened that night, I know it did." I rub the back of my neck. "What's going on?"

Zoey waves her hand in the air, dismissing me. I suddenly want to take back everything I've said up to this point. "I don't have to tell you everything, Colette. I'm allowed to have a life outside of you."

I'll admit—it hurts more than I can acknowledge.

I've always known that marriage is nothing if not erratic and complex, and I could lose Nick at any moment. But I never, ever considered I could lose Zoey too.

————

The timing is all wrong; I know it from the moment Nick looks at me that night. I don't want to tell him what happened with Zoey, don't want to give him the satisfaction of being right. So I push the memory of the last twenty minutes deep down and try to focus on the bigger issue: Nick is finally ready to continue the conversation we started over our dinner date. I have to make myself ready for it.

He's sitting on the bed, the covers folded back away from him. "I've been thinking a lot about what you said." He begins rattling off my complaints, counting them on his fingers like a kindergartner trying to do math. "You're feeling unappreciated, you're tired of telling me what needs to be done, and you think I give you the silent treatment when I'm mad."

"No. I don't think you give me the silent treatment. You do."

His Adam's apple bobs as he swallows. "Okay," he says.

He looks up from his hands at me, waiting. It takes me a moment to realize what he's waiting for.

"You want me to initiate sex more." I'm quiet, trying to remember what other concerns he raised, but memories of Zoey keep intruding. Finally, I say, "You're worried I don't have any hobbies."

"There's actually more to the sex thing," he says slowly. Of course, there is.

"Okay."

"Okay," he repeats. "It's not just about you not initiating sex."

I had figured as much.

"Regardless of who's initiating it, we simply don't... enough. I mean, do you even remember the last time we slept together?"

I don't. And I don't want to admit it either. I must look unsure because he says, "It was New Year's Eve."

My pulse quickens. "That can't be right."

"It is."

Okay, so it's bad. We're well into spring now.

"I'm not trying to put all the blame on you, Letty. I know there are two of us in this marriage. But I just want to know you still want me."

Even dressed for bed, Nick is handsome. His line of work has made him strong, thick, and tan. There's nothing special about his hair or the shape of his mouth and face, but they're arranged just so, in a way making him irresistible. It's his eyes, light brown with flecks of green, that sealed the deal for me. But my attitude toward him, toward sex, toward our marriage —it has nothing to do with how he looks. It all comes down to how I feel. But how do I make him understand?

"Your wheels are turning," he says with a slight smile.

I laugh, but the sound catches in my throat. I inhale, exhale, and then do my best to put words to what I'm feeling. "I think, for you, the act of sex is as simple as needing to feel desired. If a woman is willing, than that's enough for you. But for me, there's a lot more to it. I need to feel seen. I need to feel heard and cherished and loved. I can't be mad at you one moment and then sleep with you the next. I'm sure there are women out there who can, but I'm not one of them."

His expression is unreadable. And as a heavy silence falls over us, I realize I can't blame him for not knowing how to respond. It's one thing for me to tell him he doesn't help around the house as much as I would like, but I've essentially just admitted to not feeling seen, heard, or loved by him. I can't imagine how I would feel hearing the same from him.

"Nick…"

He looks down at his hands. "No, it's okay." He exhales heavily. "I get what you're saying." He takes one of my hands in his and lifts his eyes to mine. "I'm sorry you feel that way. And"—he rubs his thumb absentmindedly over my knuckles —"thank you for telling me. Now I can be better. I can do better."

I let myself collapse into his arms, his words releasing something inside of me. I can't say how long we stay this way, me wrapped in his arms, him lifting my hand and kissing the tips of each of my fingers like he used to when we were first married. I only know, in that moment, I feel heard and loved and safer than I have in years.

Life: 3, Colette: 3.

CHAPTER
SIXTEEN

I spent the next few days in a hope-filled daze. Nick and I finally talked—really talked. We were open and honest with each other, and while it didn't lead to sex, we held each other in a way we hadn't in a long time. It feels like a giant step in the right direction.

But now, the seed of doubt has been planted, and I'm more aware than ever of how little physical affection Nick and I have shown each other in recent years. There was a time when we couldn't keep our hands off each other. I used to know every dip and curve of his body like the back of my hand. But life got in the way, as it always does, and the time to explore each other shrank with every new responsibility— each kid, every exhausting workday, and all the family drama that came our way.

"The grass is greener where you water it," Zoey had said.

Well, Nick and I let our grass die a slow and painful death. Now, it feels like nothing but sheer willpower, a ton of fertilizer, and more rain than Las Vegas has seen in years can bring it back to life.

As the remodel progresses, I find myself thinking less and

less about the model home I once fantasized about. We've got a beautiful new kitchen where I love preparing meals, new flooring throughout the house, and my office is nearly complete. The painters are scheduled for next week, and we've painstakingly measured every window in the house to order new shades. Boxes of new door hardware are stacked in the garage, waiting for Nick to find the time to install them. The master bathroom remodel has begun, and soon we'll turn our attention to the outside of the house.

Despite all these improvements, our lack of storage remains a persistent problem. I manage to keep my worries to myself day after day, even as I kick over a stack of books next to my desk or notice the sun bleaching the cover of one of my favorite hardcovers. But really, book storage is the least of our problems. The kids' toys have taken over our linen closet, displacing towels and sheets, and I've had to get real creative with storing things like wrapping paper and old DVDs Nick insists we keep, despite not touching them in years. I'm pretty sure we still own a VHS tape of *The Little Mermaid*. I have no idea where it came from, let alone why we've held onto it.

Nick was right when he said months ago we needed to sort through everything, but that kind of time-consuming project requires the right mindset. And I just can't add this kind of purging to my already overflowing plate, no matter how necessary it might be. At one point, I considered paying Anna to help, but unless I watched her every move—which would defeat the purpose—she'd likely toss anything not connected to her directly. Like the coffee mug Ben painted for me in second grade proudly declaring, next to a stick figure drawing of himself, "MOM'S FAV KID." It's one of my favorite mugs, mostly because it makes me laugh at Ben's audacity to claim the title.

I mean—it's true. But I'd never admit it to anyone. And honestly, my feelings could change over the years. Whoever takes the most time out of their busy adult lives to call their dear old mother will probably end up as my favorite. The jury's still out on which one of my kids it'll be. Anna acts like she doesn't need me now but wait until she has her first child and realizes just how much work it really is. And Ben…well, chances are once he's married, I'll be demoted to the second most important woman in his life. As much as I might hate it, it's the way it should be.

Wait. How did I get from thinking about Nick and our sex life to my children getting married and having babies? I could have sworn that just a moment ago I was focused on something entirely different.

I swear, it's exhausting living in this head of mine.

———

As the walls in our house transform from a dingy off-white to a beautiful light gray, I start to feel open to the idea of sleeping with my husband again. It's not just the new office space or the fact that Nick has taken to cleaning different rooms without being asked. It's not even the way he suddenly seems enthralled by my work stories. These things certainly don't hurt, but mostly, I feel a change within myself.

By finally voicing our issues, I've released some of the pressure inside me. I'm no longer carrying the burden alone. Our problems—some of them, anyway—are now out in the open, and we can work on fixing them. Fixing our marriage.

But as honest as we've been with each other, there's still a long list of things I haven't brought up with Nick. And I'm sure sex and missing hobbies aren't the only things on his mind either. We have many conversations left to have. I still need to talk to him about his attitude toward the kids, which is going to be a tough discussion. And I need to address his habit of micromanaging the money I spend—though I'll admit, he's been better about it lately. I've told him I'm exhausted, yes, but I haven't gone into detail about how he contributes to it—another conversation I'm not looking forward to. But I need to water my grass. I need to tend to my marriage.

And so—I ask my husband out on a date.

———

I choose a restaurant neither of us has been to before, reasoning that a new experience will be good for us, something we can bond over. Italian seems like a safe bet, and the name, *Trattoria Reggiano*, is fun to say. *Trattoria Reggiano, Trattoria Reggiano*—it rolls off the tongue in a very satisfying way. The weather is beautiful, and I'm glad I requested a table outside. From our little two-top, we can watch residents and tourists alike scamper past on their way to and from shopping or meals of their own. The chatter of parents and the laughter of children provide the perfect soundtrack to our meal.

We go all out, ordering bruschetta, calamari, and a panzanella salad to start. I sip greedily on a limoncello spritz while Nick enjoys a pint of Stella Artois. By the time our entrées arrive—veal scaloppini piccata for Nick and spaghetti carbonara for me—we're pleasantly buzzed. Our conversation flows easily, which, after the last few months, I'm incredibly grateful for.

"I've been giving a lot of thought to what you said about finding a new hobby…and other things. I want you to know I hear you."

"I hear you." It's a line a therapist once told me to use during difficult discussions.

"Thank you for trying. That's all I ask," Nick says, adding, "I'm trying too."

I nod. "I see it. Thank you."

Thank you, no thank you—we're being so kind and sweet it's almost sickening. Probably what we need is to act out a scene or two from some sexy movie or Netflix show. The thought alone makes warmth creep up my neck.

I watch my husband of fourteen years finish his beer and order another. I take in the curve of his muscles beneath his T-shirt, the hint of a tan line along his collarbone. The grays at his temples have multiplied, but they suit him. I lift a hand to my hairline, suddenly self-conscious. It's been months since I've colored my hair. I make a mental note to book an appointment with my hairdresser as soon as possible. I haven't thought much about how I present myself to the world these last few years. Working from home means I'm usually alone. I dress up for Zoom meetings with authors and agents, but most of the time it's just me in jeans and whatever T-shirt is hanging in my closet. My hair is more or less brushed every day, but my makeup routine is minimal—a dab of concealer under my eyes, a touch of blush, and a quick flick of mascara.

I continue to watch Nick long after his second beer arrives, long after he returns his attention to me, a curious look crossing his face. Eventually, a nervous smile tugs at his mouth.

"What is it?" He hovers his hand near his mouth. "Do I have something in my teeth?"

I decide to stick with honesty. "I was just thinking about how handsome you are." I leave off the part where I criticize myself.

"Thank you," he says, his smile widening so much I can see his molars. "You're not too shabby yourself."

Sure, I look okay tonight—I've actually tried. But most other days...

"You're doing the overthinking thing again," he says, cutting through my thoughts. "You're trying to figure out if

I'm lying to you, just trying to be nice." He stops me from interrupting. "I wish you could see yourself the way I do."

Never knowing how to accept a compliment, I feel my face flush. All these years, and I still can't find a way to simply say, "Thank you."

There is, of course, one way I could show my gratitude without saying the words—*Here, let me show you my appreciation by lying down and letting you ravage me.*

It seems…fitting.

Except, the longer the night goes on, the more nervous I become. I haven't shaved my legs or put on a sexy bra. My underwear doesn't even match! Even though I know none of this would stop Nick from wanting to have sex, especially considering how long it's been, I can't quite wrap my head around the idea of it happening tonight.

It doesn't help that Nick seems to have read my mind and knows what I'm contemplating. During the drive home, he keeps his hand tucked under my thigh like he used to do when we first started dating. Back then, we were always finding ways to touch each other, even when it wasn't convenient. It was something people noticed and commented on, often with a hint of jealousy they tried to hide. The women, especially, wanted their men to act this way, to want to touch them like he so openly touched me. I never took it for granted back then, but somewhere along the line, I forgot the feeling. I forgot a lot of things.

At home, in our bedroom, I go about cleansing my face and brushing my teeth, trying to summon the thoughts I had of Nick over dinner. Trying to push aside the insecurities about how I look and feel in my body. I think of my favorite scenes from the sexy TV show, and in the closet, I slip a silk nightgown over my head. I ignore the fact it's tighter across my middle than the last time I wore it and study myself in the mirror. Deep breath and—

Nick is standing over my nightstand, the top drawer open. He seems to be looking for something.

"What are you doing?" I ask, my voice wavering. I resist the urge to move from my spot by the bathroom door.

He turns toward me, a phone charger dangling from his right hand. "Is it all right if I use this, or do you need it? I can't find mine anywhere."

I exhale slowly, the sound of my heart hammering in my ears. "Go ahead," I say. I wait for him to cross the room and plug in his phone before I move toward the nightstand. I open the drawer slowly, pretending to look for my reading glasses, which I know are safely on my desk in the office. Beneath the latest issue of *People Magazine*, various coupons, and half-used lip balms, I can just make out the corner of the legal pad. The list is safely tucked away.

I breathe a sigh of relief, though my hands are still shaking.

"Letty?" I look up to see Nick studying me, a shy smile on his face. It takes me a moment to remember the nightgown I'm wearing, the way it hugs my curves and accentuates my chest. It's short enough to show off the better part of my thighs. In the past, wearing this nightgown was meant to send a clear signal to Nick that I was in the mood to play.

Nick has picked up on my signal, and he wants to play.

He crosses the room in four short strides and presses his mouth to mine. He tastes and smells of minty toothpaste, and beneath it, the tiniest hint of the beer he had at dinner. I close my eyes, giving in to the kiss. I feel his strong hands on my jawline, his firm chest against mine. A moan escapes my lips as he guides me down onto the bed. I can't remember the last time we kissed like this, the last time we—

I have to take care of almost everything at home.

He knows little about the day-to-day details of the kids' lives.

He gives me the silent treatment when he's mad.

I wince, trying to push the intrusive thoughts away. Nick

pulls back slightly, his eyes searching mine. I circle my hands around the back of his neck, pulling him closer. His mouth finds mine again.

I always have to tell him what needs to be done around the house.

I try to seem natural as I pull away, as if I'm overcome with desire and need to catch my breath. But I know the moment I do it that I can't sleep with him. I might want to be ready to sleep with him, but I can't force something like this. I just don't have it in me.

One quick glance at my face, and Nick comes to the same conclusion.

I watch as he slowly moves away, working hard to keep his expression neutral and non-judgmental. But I know he's disappointed. And he has every right to be.

I lie next to him, eyes closed but awake, until his breathing changes and I know he's asleep.

And then I cry.

I've never felt like such a failure before. What kind of wife can't drum up the desire to sleep with the man she loves? And if I can't do this one simple thing, something meant to be pleasurable and bring us closer together, how are we ever going to fix our marriage?

CHAPTER
SEVENTEEN

I'm ashamed to admit just how much time I spend hiding in my office after my failed attempt at seduction. It's almost easier this way, to avoid facing what happened, and what it means. Nick doesn't seem to be in any rush to discuss it either, so we don't. We let the silence grow between us, filling the spaces where conversations about our marriage should be.

In a twisted way, it's perfect timing that my new office is finally complete, a sanctuary where I can disappear. The days blur together in a haze of work, renovations, and cleaning. By mid-May, the master bathroom renovation is well underway, and it feels strange having Zac working upstairs, so close to my personal space.

I'm acutely aware of him being among my things, walking past my bed day in and day out. The first time I see him in my bedroom, it feels almost sensual. He's crouched near the bathroom door, pulling up baseboard with his back to me. Music pours from a small blue speaker beside him, and I watch him work, my eyes tracing the way his muscles move—his biceps flexing, his shoulders tightening and releasing with each pull.

Sensual isn't the right word. There's only one word that fits—erotic.

The realization startles me, and I practically run from the room to escape my thoughts. But days pass, and I still can't shake the image. Why is it so easy to look at Zac and feel this way, yet so difficult to connect with my own husband? I've never been the type of woman who enjoys casual flings. I've always preferred the comfort that comes after settling into a relationship, the familiarity deepening over time. It feels wrong, on so many levels, to be thinking of Zac like this.

I start counting down the days until the remodel is complete, not because I want my house back, but because I want Zac gone. Out of sight, out of mind. Just knowing he's in my bedroom or making himself a coffee in my kitchen as I encouraged him to do, is too much. I'm feeling too much, and it scares me.

Thankfully, work has always been a reliable distraction from my worries. During the workday is the only time I can shut off the parts of my brain not devoted to publishing. Closed in my office with a fresh cup of coffee, I shut out the world. There are emails to respond to, contract terms to review, and cover copy to approve. Friday is my favorite day because everyone is preoccupied with their work, leaving me plenty of time to focus on mine without interruption.

But this morning, my solitude is interrupted by a notification from Slack—Matt is calling me into a huddle. I tuck my hair behind my ears, sit up straight, and answer the call. Matt's face appears on the screen, and I know from experience that nothing good ever follows those apologetic eyes.

"Hi Colette, I'm sorry to bother you, but I was hoping you had a moment to talk."

I smile, but my heart sinks. "Sure, Matt. What's going on?"

He exhales heavily, and I hold my breath.

"To be honest, I'm a little nervous about being moved to the thriller imprint."

"Oh," I say, forcing calm into my voice. "How come?"

"I was really happy working with the young adult titles. I'm more confident with the genre, you know? I'm nervous I don't know enough about thrillers, about the nuances and themes."

"I understand why you might feel this way," I say, my tone reassuring. "But can I tell you what I think?" I don't wait for his response. "The only reason we were confident in this transition is because we know you'll do great. We can always work on increasing your knowledge of the genre, and you'll learn best by diving in and reading some bestsellers. I can send you some titles if you'd like. But a lot of what made you successful in YA will apply here as well. So, don't second-guess yourself, Matt. We all believe in you."

Matt's face softens, dimples forming on either side of his mouth as he pulls in a quick breath. "Okay. You're right. I'm sorry for taking up your time."

I shake my head. "I'm always here if you need to talk. I appreciate you bringing your concerns to me." I tilt my head slightly. "Are we good?"

He smiles again, those dimples deepening. "We're good. Thanks, Colette."

"No problem." Crisis averted—for now.

The huddle ends, leaving the room in silence. But the sound of footsteps above me serves as a constant reminder I still have one more potential crisis to manage.

Luckily, I've had plenty of practice pretending everything is fine.

———

The weekend passes in a flurry of activity—Ben starts swim practice on Saturday morning, Anna needs a ride to and from the Summerlin Mall with her friends, and Nick and I perform a well-choreographed dance of avoidance. Before I know it, Monday morning arrives.

I'm surprised to find a new meeting on my calendar at nine a.m. Brent has always hated Mondays and refuses to schedule meetings on the first day of the week. So, imagine my shock when I see the blue box glaring at me from my Google calendar.

I barely have enough time to run upstairs, brush my hair, dab concealer under my eyes, and throw on a clean outfit before Zoom alerts me to the upcoming meeting. I sign onto the call, relieved that for the first time in years, I don't have to worry about what's behind me in the background.

I'm smiling when Brent's face appears on the screen. "Oh good," he says. "You look like you're in a good mood. It'll make this easier."

My smile falters. "What happened?"

My mind jumps to Emily—maybe she's pregnant again and planning to leave work for good. I wouldn't blame her. I had wanted to do the same when I found out we were expecting Ben, but we couldn't afford to live on one income. I was disappointed, yes, but I loved my job, and that made it easier. But before I can spiral further, Brent's voice cuts through my thoughts.

"Matt quit over the weekend."

I wince, squeezing my eyes shut. *Danger! Trouble ahead!*

"He said he spoke to you on Friday."

I sigh, reopening my eyes to focus on Brent's face. "He was doubting the move to thrillers," I nod. "But I thought we'd worked it out."

Brent's expression shifts, frustration clear. "I hate it when good kids make stupid decisions."

I feel a sudden wave of defensiveness for Matt. "Did he tell you why?"

Brent waves me off, and I'm certain now that Matt's decision wasn't a stupid one. He's a good, smart kid; he probably thought it through and wrestled with the choice. I just wish I'd done a better job convincing him to stay.

"Anyway, as you know, this leaves us with no one to cover thrillers. I don't want there to be any confusion transitioning Emily to YA, so I think it's best if you cover him for now."

A frown forms so deep on my forehead I can practically feel another wrinkle etching into my skin. "Only until we get someone trained and up to speed," Brent adds, though we both know what he really means: a long, drawn-out process of posting the job, sorting through applications, making introductory calls, conducting interviews, and then finally training the new hire. It's not a quick fix.

Most of the time, I love being part of a small team. I love the camaraderie, the teamwork, the trust, and the respect we have for one another. It's when we lose someone that the cracks begin to show. As the manager of this small team, losing Matt is now my problem to solve—essentially what Brent is trying to say.

"Yes, sir," I respond, ever agreeable, ever professional.

Brent claps his hands together, startling me. "I'll get the posting up tomorrow. In the meantime, you know what to do."

The Zoom call ends, my screen returning to the smiling faces of my family in the background. I sit there, staring at the screen as tears begin to fall, silent and unexpected. I let them come, grateful for the privacy of my office. I cry until my face is dry, until the frustration drains from my body, and then I head off in search of Zac.

I find him on his hands and knees in my master bathroom. He looks up when he notices me standing in the doorway.

"Would you like to go somewhere with me?" I ask, my voice barely above a whisper.

———

It's a completely different experience walking through the model home with someone as excited by it as I am. Zac is like a kid in a candy store, commenting on the drop ceiling accent over the island and how it draws the eye to the center of the kitchen, or the addition of the fireplace in the great room and the warmth it brings to the space. He speaks as if life itself is bright and beautiful, his enthusiasm infectious.

As we walk through the rooms, the weight of the morning's news begins to lift from my shoulders.

Before we left the house, I made us both coffees to go. Now, as we sit on the living room couches, it feels as though we're old friends catching up over coffee.

"This is still one of my favorite layouts," Zac says. I nod, thinking of the cozy café in the back corner of the house, the small den that would make the perfect office, and the laundry room with space for a wash tub and a counter to fold clothes. The idea of folding laundry fresh from the dryer, the heat tickling my arms, excites me more than anything else. My mother used to lug baskets of laundry up and down the stairs, grumbling the entire way. As a child, I watched her, and the idea of a dream laundry room cemented itself in my impressionable mind.

I sink deeper into the couch. "I love it here."

A knowing smile spreads across Zac's face. "You could still move, you know. There's no rule saying you have to stay just because you went through with the renovations."

It's the same thought I've had a hundred times.

I allow myself to imagine the kids eating breakfast at the table, Nick and I sitting on the couch watching the news,

Mayer curled up between us, purring contentedly. It's a picture-perfect fantasy that feels entirely unattainable.

But it's not just the house. It's everything—the way Anna has become a tween nightmare, the way Ben barely eats anymore but is obsessed with being tall enough to sit in the front seat, the way Nick and I can't seem to find our footing, always tilting too far one way or the other. And let's not even talk about the extra twenty pounds around my middle I can't seem to lose without actually working out.

I look at Zac. "What would you do if you were me? Would you stay and make it work, or would you go?"

"Depends on what the real question is," he says softly.

I hold my breath.

He continues, "I'm a pretty observant guy. I kind of have to be. And sometimes it extends beyond construction."

I play dumb. "What do you mean?"

"I mean, the first day we met, you mentioned how Nick always gets what he wants. Then you asked about my marriage, and why things didn't work out. And then there was that day in your office..."

He doesn't need to say more—I remember it clearly: the wetness on my cheeks, the feel of his arm around me, the sporty smell of men's deodorant and hard work.

But still, I could deny it all. I could chalk it up to being emotional, to being curious about other people's lives. None of it would be a lie. But it wouldn't be the whole truth either.

"It's complicated," I say instead.

He nods knowingly. "It always is."

A beat of silence stretches between us.

"The question," I say eventually. "It's about the house."

"Okay."

"So, would you stay or go?"

His eyes meet mine. "The house is great," he says. "I can see why you'd want to stay." He glances around the room before looking back at me. "But this house is pretty great too."

I ask again, "Would you stay or go?"

Even from across the space between us, I see his gaze hover on my mouth before darting away. I feel the heat rising along my neck.

"I'd stay," he says eventually, just as I knew he would.

We sit in silence, watching each other, until the moment grows uncomfortable.

———

By the time Nick gets home from work, I've calmed down enough to recount what happened at work without my chest tightening. He stands at the entrance to my office, his body filling the doorway. As I speak, I find myself thinking of something Zoey used to ask: *Do you want comfort or solutions?* It unnerves me to recognize I want Nick to know what I need without having to ask.

"Have you eaten?" he asks.

Around noon, I had the leftover chicken salad I found in the back of the fridge, but it was barely enough to cover a slice of toast. Still, the last thing I feel is hunger.

"I'm not really hungry."

"Kids," he bellows, startling me. "We're going out for dinner."

I start to shake my head, about to explain how I have far too much work to do, but he cuts me off. "We'll get out of your hair, give you some peace."

And that's the thing about being consistently disappointed in your partner: all it takes is one tiny glimpse of the person they used to be for all hope to come flooding back. I could kiss him for this. And I probably should—maybe it would solve a lot of our problems. But my mind is on work: on the contracts needing to be finalized and creative briefs to be written, the email I need to compose announcing yet another employee's departure. Telling authors the person they've built a relationship with is gone never gets easier, even though it happens all the time in publishing. It always feels like a tiny failure on our part—that we couldn't hold onto them. But such thoughts are a waste of time, and I know it.

Ben appears at the door with Anna trailing behind, looking anything but excited about going out for dinner. She stares down at her phone, her fingers tapping furiously on the screen.

"Anna," I say. She ignores me, so I say her name again, and a third time, until finally, she looks up, her eyes hazy and unfocused. "I'd like you to leave your phone at home when you go to dinner."

Her eyes widen. "But Mom!"

I shake my head. "You can go without it for two hours." I stand up and urge them away from the doorway. "Now off you go. Have fun." I turn my back to them, avoiding the inevitable glare from Anna, and gently shut the office door.

It'll be good for them to have some quality time with their dad, and equally good for me to have some extra time alone to catch up on work. It wouldn't be the same with them upstairs, out of sight but still present, their desire to interrupt me palpable. It's too hard to focus under those conditions, weighed down by guilt.

There's already too much in my life to feel guilty about.

———

Two hours pass in the blink of an eye, and before I know it, I hear the telltale sound of the front door slamming and the children's footsteps on the stairs. I take a deep breath and release it slowly, rising from my chair. I'm not ready for them to be home, not ready to stop working, but there's nothing I can do about it. Nick has done his part—been a good parent, and a good partner. Now it's my turn.

My office door opens just as I'm getting to my feet, and Ben's sweet face appears. He's grinning from ear to ear as he pulls his arm out from behind his back, producing a takeout container. "We brought you some dinner, Mommy," he says. I take the food from him, set it on the desk, and then pull him into a tight hug.

"Thank you so much, my love."

His smile widens, cracking my heart wide open. How lucky they are, these kids. They could never know just how much they mean to me, could never know the effect they have on me, could never know just how much I love them.

That's one truth I'll never have to pretend.

CHAPTER
EIGHTEEN

Six weeks. It's been six long, agonizing weeks since I last spoke to Zoey, since I last saw her face or heard her voice. Every day without her feels like a fresh wound, a raw, aching cut refusing to heal, festering with the weight of uncertainty and worry. I never imagined the absence of someone who has been in my life for so long could feel like this—like a part of me has been carved out, leaving a hollow space nothing else can fill. And the worst part? I don't know why. I don't know if she's okay, if she's angry with me, if she needs me as much as I need her. The silence between us has grown unbearable, like an invisible wall I keep running into but can't break through.

It feels wrong—fundamentally wrong—to be going through everything in my life without her. Every little thing, from the tensions in my marriage to the pressures of work and the constant struggles of parenting a twelve-year-old daughter, feels heavier, more unmanageable without Zoey to help me carry the load. She's always been the person I could turn to, my sounding board, my confidante. And now, with her gone, I feel lost. There's a gnawing, aching worry in the pit of my stomach that keeps growing. What is she going through without me? Is she struggling as much as I am? Is she even okay?

I think about her constantly. What must she be going through right now? I picture her in the house she shared with Aaron, alone. Has she and Aaron spoken since she told him to leave? Have they even tried to work things out, or is it really over? Have they decided to go to counseling, to try to save what's left, or is it already too late? These questions swirl in my mind every day, and they tear at me because I don't know the answers. It's killing me, this not knowing.

And what about the twins? How are they handling all of this? I picture Stella, tough and resilient, but even the strongest kids crack under pressure. And Sam…God, I worry about Sam more than anyone. He's always been such a sensitive boy, so open with his emotions, wearing his heart on his sleeve and making him more vulnerable than other kids his age. He's the kind of boy who feels deeply, who takes things to heart in a way that scares me because I know how fragile it can make him. Is he breaking down inside, watching his family fall apart? Is anyone there to comfort him, to tell him everything's going to be okay, even if it isn't?

And then there's me. I can't talk to Nick about any of this. Not really. Every time I try to bring up Zoey's absence, I see the look in his eyes, the one telling me he thinks I'm meddling, sticking my nose where it doesn't belong. He warned me not to get involved, not to interfere in Zoey's marriage, but I didn't listen. I never listen to Nick when it comes to things like this. I thought I knew better; thought I could help Zoey. But I was wrong. And now, here I am, six weeks later, with nothing to show for it except this gaping hole in my chest where my best friend used to be.

I wonder if I've learned anything over the past few months. It doesn't feel like it. Not when Nick has been making so many improvements, doing everything I've asked of him. He's been more thoughtful and engaged. He's listening to me in a way he hasn't in years, and I can see how hard he's trying. He's trying for us, for our family, and yet I'm stuck. I'm still here, repeating the same mistakes, feeling disconnected and distant. I haven't even done the one simple thing he asked me to do—find a hobby. A hobby. How hard can it be? But for some reason, I haven't made the effort. I tell myself it's because I'm too busy, too overwhelmed, but deep down, I know it's not the whole truth.

What does it say about me that I can't even make such a small change?

I don't want to know. I'm afraid to know.

I force myself to focus on the present, to ground myself in the moment. I'm in the kitchen, stirring a pot of penne in boiling water, the steam rising around me. Behind me, I can hear the kids talking with Nick at the table, their voices a soft murmur as they discuss their plans for the upcoming week. It's the last week of the school year, and somehow, I hadn't even realized how quickly the time had passed. The year has flown by, slipping through my fingers while I was too preoccupied with my own problems to notice. And now summer is almost here.

Summer. The word alone fills me with dread. The kids will be home more, with only a few weeks of camp scheduled, which means I'll be juggling them and my work with little to no break. How am I supposed to manage everything when they're here, needing my attention, pulling me in every direction? I've been so caught up in my own drama that I haven't even begun to prepare for the chaos summer will bring. It feels like everything is slipping out of my control, like the ground is shifting beneath my feet, and I don't know how to steady myself.

Everything is fine.

Matt is gone, and no one has been hired to replace him.

Everything is fine.

Anna and Ben have been unceremoniously banished from Sam and Stella's lives.

Everything is fine.

I can't bring myself to do something as basic and natural as sleep with my own husband.

Everything is fine.

And then there's Zac, who was supposed to have finished the home renovations by now. I haven't seen him in what feels like weeks, and the house is still unfinished. The ratty old banister is still here, just like I feared, and the storage problems remain unresolved. It feels like everything is falling apart, one small piece at a time.

Everything is clearly *not* fine.

The incessant beeping of the kitchen timer pulls me out of my thoughts, a harsh reminder that life keeps moving forward, even when I feel stuck. I hastily pull the pot off the burner and drain the noodles, going through the motions of dividing the pasta into bowls, and adding sauce and freshly grated parmesan on top. In a separate bowl, I toss the salad with dressing, bringing it to the table where the kids are waiting. Anna reaches over and plucks a cherry tomato from the bowl, popping it into her mouth before I've even had a chance to sit down. Ben follows suit, mimicking his sister as he often does, a small smile playing on his lips.

Nick catches my eye across the table, offering me a small, tired smile of his own. I smile back, but it's forced. It's the kind of smile that fails to reach my eyes, the kind of smile that doesn't fool anyone. I know by the way Nick looks at me that he can see through it. He knows I'm not really okay. But neither of us says anything. We just go through the motions, pretending.

Dinner passes in a blur of quiet conversation and clinking forks. I barely speak unless someone addresses me directly, the cloud hanging over my head growing heavier with each passing minute. By the time we're done, I feel like I'm suffocating under the weight of it all.

And then, out of nowhere, it hits me.

I don't want to be here.

Not just at this table, not just in this kitchen, but here, in this life. The realization sends a jolt of fear through me. I don't want this life. I don't want to be here. The thought is terrifying, but I can't shake it.

———

Later that week, when Nick comes home from work, he's practically glowing with excitement. I hear the door open and close, and a few moments later, he appears in the doorway of my office, smiling so wide I can see his molars. His face is flushed, his hair slightly damp from the heat of the day. He looks younger and happier than I've seen him in a long time. I want to match his energy, but I'm too tired, too drained.

"Hey," I say, trying to sound more upbeat than I feel. "How was your day?"

"Good. Really good," he says, stepping into the room. "Are you almost done for the day?"

I glance at my computer screen, the long list of unfinished tasks glaring back at me. "I've still got a few things to wrap up," I say, though my heart isn't in it. "Why?"

Nick taps his knuckles against the doorframe, his excitement palpable. "I've got something planned for us tonight. I think you'll like it."

A knot forms in my stomach. Whatever he has planned, I'm not in the mood. But I want to be. I want to show up for him, to be the wife he needs. So I force a smile and nod. "Okay. Just give me a few minutes."

When Nick steps out of the bathroom, the scent of his

aftershave—fresh, clean, with a hint of citrus—hits me first. It's different from his usual smell, which catches me off guard. I glance up and almost don't recognize him. He's wearing athletic shorts and a fancy shirt I've never seen before. I stare at him for a moment, unable to stop myself from shaking my head slightly. Nick in Lululemon? When did that happen? I feel a flicker of curiosity—when did he have time to go shopping, and what prompted this sudden shift in his style? It nags at me briefly, a distraction from the constant hum of everything else swirling in my mind.

He looks good. Really good. I remind myself to focus on this fact. On him. It's been a long time since I allowed myself to truly *see* him. The way his broad shoulders fill out the shirt, the way his skin still glistens faintly from the shower. There's a softness to his smile tonight that's been missing lately, an excitement in his eyes I haven't seen in months. Maybe even longer. I try to mirror it, to feel something beyond the numbness creeping into every corner of our marriage.

I tell myself to focus on this. I *need* to focus on this, on him, on us—so hard it might kill me.

But nothing could have prepared me for what he had planned.

When Nick tells me he's taking me to a trapeze class, my jaw literally drops. I can't even mask the shock. He grins, clearly enjoying my reaction, but I feel like the ground just shifted beneath me. *A trapeze class?* Where is this coming from? I try to recover, try to plaster on a smile as I retreat into the bathroom to change into my workout clothes. I stare at myself in the mirror for longer than I should, gripping the edge of the sink like it's the only thing keeping me upright.

It's not just the trapeze class that has me rattled—it's this sudden version of Nick, this person I don't quite recognize. I look down at the leggings I'm pulling on and realize they're tighter than they were last year. Another reminder of how much has changed, how much I've changed. The workout shirt feels clingy and uncomfortable, but I force myself into it anyway. I glance at myself one last time in the mirror, giving myself a pep talk, telling myself I can do this. This is what our marriage needs—something new, something unexpected. But even as I lace up my sneakers by the front door, I feel a knot of anxiety tightening in my stomach.

When the babysitter, Lucy, arrives, she's carrying a stack of textbooks, her face etched with stress. I recognize the look all too well.

"Finals coming up?" I ask, trying to sound lighthearted. She nods, her expression bleak. "Don't worry, you'll get through it. Just breathe. You're smart, and you've got this."

She gives me a grateful smile, and for a moment, I almost envy her. The simplicity of school stress seems so far removed from the complexities of adult life—marriage, kids, a house that feels like it's falling apart, and a best friend who's been AWOL for six weeks.

Nick appears beside me, and my attention shifts back to him. He's practically buzzing with excitement. I notice again how good he looks. There's something undeniably attractive about his energy tonight, this childlike enthusiasm I hadn't seen in so long. Maybe this is what makes me nervous. His excitement makes me feel like I'm the one lagging behind, like I'm not matching his pace.

We arrive at the trapeze class, and I watch in stunned silence as Nick climbs the ladder to the 25-foot platform without a second thought. For someone who has always claimed to hate heights, he's acting fearless. He leaps off the platform, gripping the trapeze bar like he's done it a thousand times before. My heart hammers in my chest as I watch him swing, each attempt more confident than the last. By the second try, he's hanging by his knees, something I can't even fathom doing. By the fourth, he nearly makes a catch, and when he finally nails it on his fifth attempt, he beams with pride.

I, on the other hand, am a mess of awkward limbs and nerves. My hands feel slippery on the bar, my heart pounding as I swing, trying to summon the strength to hang upside down as Nick did. I barely manage a knee hang on my third and fourth attempts, and by the end, I'm exhausted—mentally and physically. But I'll give him this: the adrenaline rush is real. For a fleeting moment, I understand why Nick wanted to do this. It's exhilarating, terrifying, and freeing all at once.

As we walk back to the car, Nick reaches out and takes my hand. His palm is warm, and the simple act of him holding my hand sends a ripple of unexpected warmth through me. I feel connected to him in a way I haven't in months. Maybe even years. I squeeze his hand back, surprised by the emotion swelling in my chest.

"Thanks for being a good sport," he says, his voice soft as we cross the parking lot. "I know that was a little out of your comfort zone."

I smile, even though my mind is already racing ahead. "How did you even come up with a trapeze class of all things?"

He laughs, glancing at me sideways. "I wish I could take credit, but it was Zac's idea."

I feel a jolt of surprise, almost a physical reaction. *Zac?* The thought of Nick and Zac discussing me sends an uncomfortable shiver down my spine. I didn't realize they'd been talking much, let alone about me. "How did it come up?"

Nick unlocks the car, holding the passenger door open for me before sliding into the driver's seat. "He asked how you were liking the house now that the renovations are mostly done. I guess it got us talking about hobbies."

I slip into the seat, trying to process this new information. Zac, of all people, offering advice about hobbies? Something about it doesn't sit right, but I push the thought aside. "So, this was your attempt to get me out of the house?" I ask, keeping my tone light, forcing a smile to match.

"Something like that."

We pull onto Sunset, and I'm suddenly hyper-aware of the world outside the car. The Strip is alive with tourists, as it always is, but tonight it feels even more chaotic—people spilling out of casinos, clutching oversized drinks, laughing too loudly. They move with a sense of carefree abandon so foreign to me now. Nick and I weave through the crowd in our car, sidestepping the vendors hawking their fliers and the women dressed in skimpy outfits hoping to catch attention. We've seen it all before; it doesn't faze us anymore. But tonight, it feels like another reminder of how disconnected I've become from the world.

"This trapeze class..." I start, my voice trailing off. "Is this going to be a regular occurrence?"

Nick chuckles, the sound warm and genuine. "Not exactly. Unless you want it to be."

I shake my head, feeling a small laugh escape my lips despite myself. "No, I think once was enough. But any other wild plans I should know about? Are we going to jump off the Stratosphere next? Or maybe you've signed me up for pole dancing lessons?"

Nick grins, reaching over to take my hand again. "If you want to take pole dancing classes, I'll be nothing if not supportive."

His words make me smile, but my mind is already wandering. I think of the conversation I had with Zac, and his casual suggestions that I try yoga, or dance classes. I didn't take him seriously at the time, brushing off his advice like it didn't matter. But now, it feels like those words are echoing in my head, louder than before.

We merge onto the I-215, heading west toward home. Nick falls into his usual quiet focus behind the wheel, and I feel a sense of relief wash over me. I need the silence. My thoughts are spinning, racing ahead to the work waiting for me tomorrow, the looming summer break, the unfinished renovations. The memory of swinging through the air just an hour ago is fading fast, replaced with images of Ben's LEGOs scattered across the floor, the linen closet bursting at the seams, the endless clutter multiplying no matter how many times I try to organize it.

The house looks great on the surface, but underneath, I still feel the disappointment. Nick didn't take my need for storage seriously, and every time I walk past the cluttered corners, I feel like I'm talking to a wall. Why is it he listens to everything else but this?

"What are you thinking?" Nick's voice breaks through the silence, his eyes glancing at me as we slow to a stop at the exit ramp.

I stare straight ahead, trying to will the earlier feeling of excitement back. I try to remember the rush of the trapeze bar in my hands, the brief moment of weightlessness as I swung through the air. But it's already slipping away. "Nothing," I say, but it's a lie. And I know Nick knows it's a lie.

At this moment, I hate myself. I hate how I haven't grown and I'm still stuck in the same place I've been for months. I hate that I can't even be honest with my husband, can't tell him I want to move, and I need something to change.

And then Zac's words come back to me, unbidden: *For what it's worth, I see and hear a lot working in people's homes. There's a lot of love in this house.*

I desperately want him to be right.

CHAPTER
NINETEEN

No sooner do we pay the babysitter and send her on her way than Nick pulls me aside, his hand resting gently on my elbow. His brow is furrowed with concern, and the intensity in his eyes catches me off guard, making my breath hitch. For a moment, I forget I know exactly what he's worried about.

"What's going on?" he asks, his voice gentle but probing.

I feign ignorance, even though I know it's pointless. "What do you mean?"

His mouth twitches in a half-smile that doesn't quite reach his eyes. "Letty, come on. One second you're happy, holding my hand, and the next you're silent, completely withdrawn. You barely said a word once we got in the car. Tell me what's going on."

But I'm not ready to unpack the mess in my head, not ready to spill everything I've been bottling up. "I'm not ready," I say quietly, turning away before I have to see the disappointment flicker across his face.

Nick hesitates like he wants to push but decides against it. He sighs, and the silence between us grows heavy, the weight of everything unsaid pressing down on both of us. We change into our pajamas and climb into bed, the air between us thick with unspoken words.

It isn't until we're lying side by side, facing opposite walls, that he finally speaks again.

"I have another thing I'd like to ask of you," he says, his voice low and cautious, as though he's stepping into dangerous territory.

I close my eyes, dread washing over me. I can't handle another request. Not tonight. Not after everything.

Nick doesn't wait for me to respond. "I want you to be more open with me. You're keeping things bottled up, and it's making everything worse."

I turn away from him, shaking my head. "You don't want to hear everything going on in my head, believe me." I mean it too. My thoughts are messy, tangled up in doubts, guilt, and frustrations I've only just begun to sort through. Hell, Zoey has been treating me like garbage, pulling away when she should be leaning on me, and what have I done about it? Nothing. I've just let it happen, absorbing it all like I always do.

So much for my supposed kindness and loyalty.

I can feel Nick watching me, his concern practically radiating off him. "Every thought? No. But if it's something I deserve to hear, I think you should tell me."

His words hit a nerve, and a surge of irritation rises in my chest. How am I supposed to know what he "deserves" to hear? Does he deserve to know how much I miss Zoey? How terrified I am of Anna pulling away? That I think about Zac more than I should? Does he deserve to know how much guilt I carry for not initiating sex even though I know how much it matters to him?

One thing is for certain; I'm starting to regret ever suggesting we be more honest with each other. Honesty is a double-edged sword, and right now, it's cutting us both to pieces. Sure, we're still sleeping in the same bed, but I've never felt so far away from him.

"I'm serious," Nick presses, his voice firm but not unkind. "I can't help if you don't let me in."

I'm trying, I want to say, but the words stick in my throat.

It would be easy to bring up the unfinished renovations. Doesn't he deserve to know about my frustration with the house, and the half-finished projects still looming over us? But I already know how he'll react. It's not what he's asking for. He's looking for something deeper, something rawer. He wants me to dig into the parts of myself I'm not ready to share.

I sigh heavily, turning over to face him. "It's not that simple."

Nick's expression softens, but his eyes are still searching mine. "It doesn't have to be, Letty. Just…start somewhere."

I glance at him, the words I want to say bubbling up, but I swallow them down. It would have been easier if I'd just slept with him already, if I'd given him the connection he so desperately craves. Maybe then we wouldn't be here, teetering on the edge of something I'm afraid we won't be able to fix.

———

The next evening, just as I'm shutting down my computer and mentally preparing to make dinner, a huddle request pops up on my screen. I sigh, clicking "Join" before I even have time to think about it, and Brent's unshaven, relaxed face fills my screen. His easygoing demeanor immediately puts me on edge.

"I know you're busy, Colette, so I'll keep this quick," he begins, and I brace myself. "I need you to look at the YA back-list. A lot of titles have outdated keywords and subtitles. We're missing out on exposure, and I'd prefer you handle it. I'm worried Emily might need too much hand-holding."

I want to say no. I have every right to. The YA imprint is Emily's responsibility, and she's perfectly capable of handling it. But instead, I bite back my frustration and say, "I'll get started on it as soon as possible."

"Perfect. You're saving my ass here, Colette. I appreciate it."

As soon as I end the call, I notice Nick standing in the doorway, watching me. His arms are crossed, his expression unreadable.

"What?" I ask, my voice betraying the exhaustion I feel deep in my bones.

"What?" he repeats, his tone mimicking mine.

"You're staring at me."

Nick sighs, dropping his gaze to the floor before looking back at me. "You're allowed to say no, you know."

A bitter laugh escapes me before I can stop it. "If only it were so simple."

He frowns. "It should be."

I push back from my desk, standing and stretching my back. "There's no one else to do it, Nick. It's unfair, but it's true."

Nick's quiet for a moment, considering this, but then he shakes his head. "I don't buy it."

I look at him, narrowing my eyes. "You don't have to understand it."

"What's that supposed to mean?" he asks, his tone sharper now, his frustration starting to show.

The words slip out before I can stop them. "Nothing. I didn't mean anything by it."

"Don't do that," Nick says, stepping into the room, his voice firm. "Say it. Stop bottling it up."

I sigh, my head falling forward. "Not this again, please."

Nick steps closer, his voice softening. "Letty, I'm just asking you to be honest with me. You wanted honesty, remember? Or is it too uncomfortable now?"

The frustration inside me bubbles over, and before I can stop myself, the words come spilling out.

"Fine," I say, my voice rising. "If we're being honest, I want to know how you think the renovations are done when we still have that awful banister and haven't solved the storage issue. The whole reason we started this in the first place was because we needed more space."

Nick's face falls, and I instantly regret my tone. "What you've done so far is beautiful, Nick, but it's not *finished*. And it hurts that you thought we were done. It makes me feel like you weren't really listening."

The hurt in his eyes is unmistakable, and the silence following is heavy and tense. I keep talking, desperate to fill the void, to ease the guilt gnawing at me.

"That's not all, either. I miss Zoey so much it's making me sick. She's pulling away from me, and it's driving me insane. And Anna—she's pushing me away too, and even though I know it's normal, it still hurts like hell. But somehow, you manage to brush it off like it doesn't matter. I can't do it, Nick. I absorb everything—the work stress, the kids, Zoey, our issues. I take it all in, and I don't know how to let it go."

My voice cracks, and I swallow hard, trying to keep the tears at bay. "Is that what you wanted to hear? Do you feel better now? Because I sure don't."

And before I can stop myself, I do the most immature thing imaginable—I turn and walk out on him, something we both swore we'd never do.

———

I'm lucky Nick follows me. Lucky that in this moment, he respects our marriage more than I do.

In the bedroom, I lie down on the bed, facing the wall, my body tense. Nick sits beside me, tucking one leg under himself, the other dangling off the bed.

"Why do you insist on holding everything in?" he asks, his voice softer now. "I'm your partner, Letty. You can talk to me about anything, anytime. I thought you knew."

The shame hits me like a tidal wave. "Everything I'm going through…all these thoughts, all these mistakes I've made…it just reminds me I'm failing. No, *flailing*. And I'm so tired of feeling this way. I'm exhausted."

This time, when Nick reaches for me, I don't pull away. I let him wrap his arms around me, let myself sink into him, letting his warmth surround me.

Part of me is terrified I'll never feel this close to him again, but for now, I let that fear drift away.

"What can I do to help?" he asks softly.

"I don't know," I whisper, tears welling in my eyes. "I really don't know."

Nick presses a kiss to my temple and pulls away gently. "Okay. You'll tell me when you figure it out?"

I nod, too overwhelmed to speak.

He stands, running a hand through his hair. "For now, I'll get started on dinner."

I close my eyes, letting the quiet settle over me. But it's not long before Ben comes to get me for dinner.

Nick has made the kids' favorite—homemade mac and cheese. Anna is at the table, drowning her noodles in buffalo wing sauce, turning the whole plate a fiery red.

"Anna, easy," I say, unable to stop myself.

She rolls her eyes, the motion exaggerated.

"You can go to your room if you're going to be like that," I snap.

"I literally didn't say anything," she retorts, her tone sharp.

I mimic her voice, my frustration boiling over. "You literally rolled your eyes."

Anna glares at me, her expression defiant. "You're getting mad about sauce, Mom."

I glance at Nick for support, but he stays silent, his eyes downcast. His silence only fuels my anger. "No, I'm mad because you're acting like a spoiled brat."

Anna doesn't flinch. "Sauce, Mom," she repeats, her voice dripping with sarcasm.

For the love of... "Go to your room."

She stands, throwing a pointed look at her father who remains silent, then storms off, stomping each step deliberately loud.

I stab my fork into my pasta, my appetite gone, avoiding Nick's gaze even though I can feel him watching me.

I absorb it all.

CHAPTER
TWENTY

I once read a quote that stuck with me: "The only people who get upset when you start setting boundaries are the ones who benefited from you having none." It hits home now, after weeks of working late on Brent's backlist updates. I've been ignoring my family, surviving on coffee and leftovers, and generally wearing myself down to the point of collapse. When I finally finish the project, my body, having had enough, retaliates with the mother of all sinus infections. It forces me to spend days in bed, working in short spurts, with a cold cloth draped over my eyes to keep the light at bay.

During the hazy downtime, the quote keeps echoing in my head. By the time I'm well enough to return to my office, I've made a decision: I need to start setting boundaries—real ones. Not just for myself, but for my family too.

The problem is I've never been good at boundaries, which is likely why I've been taken advantage of so often. My first step is simple but significant—no more work past five p.m. I've already learned my lesson after snapping at Anna over something as trivial as buffalo wing sauce. Instead of retreating, I'll lean in. I'll focus on repairing what's frayed, one day, one scowl, one eye roll at a time.

It doesn't take long for the change to be noticed.

One rare evening, with the kids in bed early and summer break keeping them entertained, Nick and I find ourselves alone in our room. He sets down his book, turns to me, and reaches for my hand. "I see what you're doing," he says quietly. "I just wanted you to know I see it."

I set aside my phone, where—no, I'm not checking work emails, I swear—and give him my full attention. "Thank you," I say.

The silence between us feels warm and intimate. I focus on the feel of my hand in his, taking in the familiar lines of his face—the unshaven jaw, the light brown eyes flecked with a green that still makes me weak. Then, I lean in and kiss him.

He tastes faintly of the beer he had with dinner, but it doesn't matter. I deepen the kiss, moving closer. A soft moan escapes his lips, his hand sliding to the back of my neck, pulling me in.

When he pulls away, his breath is ragged, his eyes filled with unspoken need. *I want this*, they say. But there's something more, something vulnerable—*Please don't play with me.*

I kiss him again, pressing my hips to his. I can feel his response, and suddenly, nothing else exists. Just us. Just this moment. He pulls my shirt over my head, his lips trailing down my chest, my stomach, my thighs. For once, I'm not self-conscious about the extra weight around my middle. I'm here, fully present, as he dips between my legs and every thought disappears.

The next morning, Nick is a new man. He's up before me, making breakfast for the kids, brewing coffee, sneaking playful touches when no one's looking. I glance at him over the rim of my mug, raising an eyebrow. He grins, biting his lower lip in a way that sends another ripple of heat through me. Twice in twenty-four hours? My long-dormant parts are waking up.

Anna, engrossed in TikTok on her phone, surprises me by saying, "I saw that."

Taking a risk, I walk over and wrap my arms around her from behind. She doesn't pull away, so I breathe in her scent, my first baby, growing up too fast. Still no resistance, so I press a quick kiss to her temple. "It's good for you to see your mom and dad love each other," I say softly.

"Good" is an understatement. I hadn't realized how much I missed witnessing real love until I saw it between Nick's parents, Mike and Joan Dawson. Married for forty-five years, they're still affectionate, still finishing each other's sentences, still leaving love notes next to the coffee pot every morning. Joan had shown me a collection of Mike's notes once, saying, "I want to show you what a real husband is like."

I've never forgotten those words. They made me see my parents' relationship in stark contrast—cold, distant, devoid of affection or respect. It's Mike and Joan who've taught me what a marriage should look like. Now it's up to Nick and me to set an example for our kids.

Finally, Anna pulls away with a groan. "Gross."

"You think that now, but someday you'll appreciate it."

She doesn't look up from her phone, just mutters, "Whatever," before eyeing her plate. "Can I go?"

Nick clears her plate and turns to Ben. "What about you, bud?"

Ben ignores him and looks at me. "What does 'appreciate' mean?"

I sit beside him. "It means recognizing the worth of something, being grateful for it."

His plate is the usual half-eaten mishmash: apples, a banana, almonds he won't touch, toast. He's eating next to nothing these days, but Nick clears his plate without comment. I remind myself of Zoey's words: *They won't let themselves starve.* Apparently, Nick was the same way as a kid, and he turned out fine.

After breakfast, Nick joins Ben and me at the table with a fresh cup of coffee in hand and mentions Zac is coming over to tear out the banister. "I wanted it to be a surprise, but I thought you'd appreciate a warning this time."

I smile at him, then at Ben. "Thanks, I do appreciate it."

I sit there at the table with my two boys until my coffee mug is empty, and I'm just headed upstairs for a shower when the doorbell rings. I'm shocked to see Sam and Stella standing there, smiling, as if the weeks of forced separation have been just as hard on them.

"Hi, guys! What's going on?"

"Can we hang with you guys for a bit? Dad has us for the day but got called into an emergency meeting."

I look past the kids, and indeed, Aaron is standing sheepishly on the sidewalk. He lifts a hand in greeting but keeps his distance.

It's clear Zoey doesn't know they're here.

Still, I find myself saying, "They can stay as long as they like."

In the moments before he smiles and turns away, I cast my eyes across him, studying his face and body language for anything that might tell me what's going on between him and Zoey, but the man gives away nothing. He's a brick wall.

After Aaron leaves, I get the kids settled, though my thoughts remain tangled in Zoey's words. *You've got your own family to worry about.* She's right. I have to focus on my family first, and yet...I can't shake the worry that she needs me. But how can I be there for her when she's shut me out so completely?

I'm pulled out of my thoughts when Sam darts past me, leaving behind a cloud of teenage body odor so thick it makes me gasp.

Upstairs, under the bathroom sink, I find an extra bar of soap, some deodorant, and body wash. I work quietly for the next few hours, distracted, but when lunchtime rolls around, I make my move.

Sam is the first to arrive in the kitchen. I hand him a small bag.

"What's this?" he asks, confused.

I lean in, lowering my voice like it's some shared secret. "Just a few things for you to take home. You know, your body changes as you get older, and sometimes you need to switch up how you take care of yourself." I try to make it sound casual, even giving him an encouraging wink. His eyes widen in horror, but he nods, taking the bag. It's left by the front door as he rushes out to rejoin the others, but I consider the mission a success.

———

Later that night, I'm yanked from sleep by the sound of Anna screaming.

Nick is out of bed before I even register what's happening, his bare feet pounding down the stairs. By the time I catch up, he's standing shirtless at the bottom of the staircase, trying to calm Anna, who's in full meltdown mode. A shattered glass lies at her feet.

"No one move," I instruct, racing to grab the broom.

Anna is furious. As she pieces together what happened, her anger grows. "I woke up thirsty, and I came down to get water, but I forgot the banister was gone! I could've broken my leg—or worse!"

"It's not that bad," I say, starting to sweep up the glass, doing my best to ignore the hysterics. As far as I can tell, only her ego is hurt.

But Anna's not done. "This whole renovation is insane! There's dust everywhere, strange men constantly in and out, and now this? Why do we even need to do all this? The only thing that's changed is Mom has an office now!"

Her words sting more than I let on. I keep my head down, sweeping. There's so much I want to say, so much bubbling beneath the surface, but I bite my tongue. Now isn't the time.

"And I still have to share a bathroom with Ben!" she continues. "Couldn't we just have moved to a bigger place?"

I exchange a glance with Nick, who's remained quiet through Anna's tirade. His jaw clenches, but he stays silent. We both know there's no point arguing with her right now.

Once she storms back to her room and the glass is cleaned up, I crawl back into bed next to Nick. I open my mouth to speak but stop myself. We both know what I'm thinking, and neither of us needs to say it out loud. We'll get through this. We always do.

———

The next morning, I wake to the usual chaos of summer break. Nick is already downstairs with the kids, and I can hear the hum of Zac's tools as he works on the stairs. I take a deep breath, grateful for the few moments of quiet before facing the day.

When I come down, I find Nick in the kitchen, cleaning up after breakfast. He smiles as I enter, and it's one of those rare, effortless moments of connection. For a second, everything feels simple again, like it used to. We're in this together.

Just as I'm about to steal a quiet moment with him, the doorbell rings. It's Stella and Sam again, back for the second day in a row. They bound into the house, eager to spend time with Anna and Ben. I'm happy to see them, but it's clear Aaron is dropping them off on the sly, and once again, Zoey doesn't know.

Aaron lingers at the edge of the driveway, waiting for my reaction. He looks weary, like he's carrying the weight of the world on his shoulders. I hesitate for a moment, wondering if I should say something, but instead, I just wave him off.

As the day passes, I find myself torn. Part of me wants to reach out to Zoey, to try and bridge the gap between us, but her words play over in my mind. *Stay out of my business.* I know she meant it, but I also know how much she's struggling. How do I balance being a friend with respecting her boundaries?

When the kids finally settle down, I head upstairs, my mind swirling. I'm trying to get some work done when I hear Nick call out from downstairs, reminding me Zac will need to finish up soon.

Before I know it, the day slips away, and it's bedtime. But just as I'm drifting off to sleep, I'm jolted awake by a loud crash. I sit up in bed, my heart pounding, only to find Nick already racing toward the stairs. I follow him down, my mind half-asleep but alert.

Anna is at the bottom of the stairs, furious once again. "I tripped over the stupid tools Zac left!" she cries. I can see the anger simmering in her, the frustration at this whole renovation process bubbling over. But I can't do anything except stand there, exhausted, as Nick gently ushers her back to bed.

Once the house is finally quiet again, Nick and I crawl back into bed. He wraps an arm around me, and we lay there in silence, both of us wide awake but too tired to speak. It doesn't matter anyway. We know what the other is thinking.

We're tired. Stretched thin. But we'll keep going, keep doing what needs to be done, for each other and our family.

As I drift off to sleep, I can't help but think about Zoey again, about all the things left unsaid between us. I wonder if I'll ever get the chance to fix things, or if I've already crossed the line. I'm not sure where that leaves us, but I know one thing for sure: I'm not done fighting for the people I care about.

CHAPTER
TWENTY-ONE

For days, I've been waking up, feeling far from ready to face the day. It doesn't matter how early I fall asleep the night before—it never feels like enough. There was a time when I would spring out of bed, eager to start the day, when my children's faces lit up the moment I entered the room. A time when they were easy to entertain, easy to please... when *I* was easier to please.

Now, I barely recognize the woman staring back at me in the bathroom mirror. This woman has faint bags under her eyes, dark spots scattered across her cheeks and nose, and dry skin clinging to her temples. My hair, oily and stuck to my face, hangs in a disheveled mess. I've been exhausted for years, but now, I *look* it.

I step into the shower, letting the hot water run over me longer than I usually would. I shave my legs, underarms, and even my bikini line—something I haven't bothered with in ages. I use the fancy hair mask Zoey gave me a couple of years ago, the one gathering dust at the back of the cupboard. The bathroom fills with the bright, citrusy scent of oranges, and for a moment, with my eyes closed, I can pretend there's nothing else for me to do but be right here.

But my moment doesn't last. Anna storms into the bathroom, demanding to know if I've seen her mascara. I didn't even know she *had* mascara, let alone wore it. I'm about to tell her this but pause. There are rare moments when you're given the chance to rise above and become what every parent hopes to be—the cool parent. I recognize I'm being handed one of those opportunities right now.

I step out of the shower, wrap a towel around my waist as Anna scrunches her face in mock disgust, and open the middle drawer of the makeup organizer by the sink. I pull out my favorite mascara—the one I caved in and bought after being bombarded with Instagram ads despite its outrageous price. Her eyes widen as she realizes what I'm about to do.

"Just make sure you bring it back when you find yours," I say, fully aware I'll never see the tube again.

"Thanks, Mom."

Her smile is worth more than a thousand cups of coffee, more than a month on a tropical beach. That smile makes me feel alive.

Suddenly, I'm wide awake.

———

A few hours later, the doorbell rings. Even with the office door closed, I recognize Zac's voice immediately. Ignoring the jolt running through me—a warning sign to STAY CLEAR I should probably heed—I'm out of my chair and in the kitchen before he's even fully stepped inside.

"You ready for the new banister?" I hear him ask Nick, who mumbles something before heading out to work, not even glancing in my direction.

Zac's footsteps echo in the hall, and then he's in the kitchen. His smile when he spots me is *everything*.

"Morning, Zac. Just grabbing a refill. You want one?" I already know his answer and am reaching for a clean mug from the drying rack.

"Never say no to coffee," he says, grinning. "Goes against my principles."

I hand him his cup and sit at the table, thrilled when he joins me, pulling out the chair across from mine. Up close like this, I notice details I've missed before—the streaks of gray in his hair, the deep laugh lines around his eyes. As we chat—about everything and nothing at all—I find myself studying him. His hazel eyes shift from almost yellow to a deep green as the light changes. His T-shirt, a faded bluish-gray, stretches across his chest as he leans back, his biceps flexing slightly with the movement.

I blink, slowly, and wonder—just for a second—what it would feel like to lean across the table and press my lips to his.

———

My chat screen with Zoey is a sea of blue bubbles, message after message—evidence of my weakness over the past ten weeks. When I'm feeling strong, I understand her need for space. But when confusion takes over, I reach out, hoping today will be the day she finally replies.

But she doesn't. Zoey ignores my messages, determined to prove her strength.

I keep trying. *I miss you*, I write. *Please talk to me.*

Nothing. No bouncing dots. No sign she's even reading them. Maybe she's blocked my number. I could call and find out, but I'm not sure I could handle it if she has.

I stare at the screen, willing her to respond. I need her—

her advice, her understanding, even her tough love. I need her to knock some sense into me, to tell me to stay in my lane, or water my own garden, or whatever it was she said that time. Maybe if I'd listened more carefully, we wouldn't be in this mess. I wouldn't be fantasizing about the contractor in my house or facing my problems with Nick and Anna on my own.

I'm losing my grip, and I need Zoey to pull me back in.

I still don't know what I did that was so wrong. Cleaning her kitchen and doing laundry couldn't be why she shut me out. There has to be something I'm missing. If she'd just talk to me, I could figure it out, apologize, and we could move past this. We used to tell each other everything. This kind of closeness doesn't just go away.

Sure, her last words to me were a little harsh—*I don't have to tell you everything, Colette. I'm allowed to have a life outside of you*—but I'm not holding it against her. I hate to admit there's truth in her statement.

I *do* feel entitled to know everything about her life. I thought our friendship worked this way. I know I can tell her anything, and she'll never judge me. She's my ride-or-die. The thought that I may have it wrong is a pill I can't swallow.

Anna's voice pulls me from my thoughts. She's standing in the doorway, glued to her phone as usual.

I swallow my irritation. "Yeah, Banana?"

Her eyes narrow at the use of her old nickname, a term of endearment from when her laughter used to fill the house. I'd give anything to hear her laugh again.

"Can you drop me at Downtown Summerlin? All the girls are going."

"Can you look at me when you ask me a question?"

She sighs and repeats her request, locking her phone and sliding it into her back pocket.

"What's so important that you can't put your phone

down?" I ask, though I know the answer. I get the pull of being constantly connected, but it doesn't mean I want my kids to make the same mistake. Look up, I want to tell them. The world is happening all around you. But I know it's no use.

Anna makes a show of locking her phone away. "It's nothing."

And just like that, I see what's really bothering me. She used to come to me with her questions about life, boys, everything. She'd sit at the foot of my bed, waiting for answers. If I'd known how quickly those moments would disappear, I would've memorized every detail. Now, all I have is a memory of a memory.

These days, she talks to her friends. I hear her giggling over her phone, and I know they're texting about boys, school, or TikTok.

It's probably because of this, because of the ghost of those memories, that I stand up and grab my keys.

"I'll take you and your friends to the mall," I say, pushing the emails and deadlines from my mind.

I need to show her she can still come to me, that I'm still here. And I need to remind myself her growing independence, though painful, is a sign Nick and I are doing something right. Even if it hurts.

CHAPTER
TWENTY-TWO

As it turns out, I don't have the patience for painting—or the talent, really—and yoga requires a level of balance and focus I sorely lack. It only takes watching the last five minutes of the beginners' intro to hip-hop class before mine is set to begin to know it isn't for me either. I'm still unwilling to try bird-watching, stamp collecting, calligraphy, or any of the strange hobbies Zac came up with months ago. I figure even if I haven't quite found my *thing*, Nick can clearly see I'm trying—which feels like a win, considering he seems to have stopped improving on his own issues.

I don't know why it has to be this way with us, why we can't be more calm, predictable, and steady. Instead, we seem to move two steps forward only to stumble one step back—over and over again. We're good, and then we're not, making love one night and going to sleep angry the next. The whole thing is giving me whiplash.

And without Zoey's help, I still haven't been able to banish Zac from my thoughts. He appears without warning as I proofread cover copy, interrupting my focus. I see his face in an author's over Zoom. A voice sounding like his stops me in my tracks at the grocery store. Once I swear I see him turn in front of me, his work truck slowly disappearing in my rearview mirror, but I chalk it up to hallucinations caused by extreme stress, which I'm now facing daily.

I've been struggling with work before, but I'm pretty sure taking over Matt's workload while simultaneously restricting my hours may have been the worst decision I've ever made—even worse than the time I got bangs in tenth grade. I stupidly thought that working shorter hours just meant I needed to be more focused during the day.

That's my first mistake.

The second is not anticipating my own husband might not make it any easier on me.

"We're out of coffee?" I ask, even as I stare at the empty canister in my hand on Thursday morning. Nick is moving around the kitchen as though his pants are on fire, a to-go cup in hand. I look at it longingly.

"I'll pick some up on the way home tonight."

"That doesn't help me now," I mutter, hoping he hears me but also glad he doesn't. "What time do you think you'll be home?"

He has a funny look on his face, which I register with trepidation. "I'm not sure yet. I'll text you."

"You've been home late all week," I gently remind him.

His back is to me. "I know."

My eyes bore into the back of his freshly shaved head—he's gotten a haircut recently, I now see. "We haven't had dinner as a family all week."

"I know," he says again, his voice flat.

I have a sinking feeling in my gut, one I would—if recent history is any indicator—normally brush aside and ignore, but Nick has told me to be more open with him, and so, I try to be.

I wait until he turns to face me. "What's going on?"

"Nothing."

Nothing, my ass. "Nick."

"I've been busy, that's all. Will has been out of town a lot." He approaches me and places a chaste kiss on my lips. "I've got to go. I'll text you when I have an idea of when I might be home."

I nod, as it's all my brain is capable of doing, considering the current onslaught of unhelpful thoughts and scenarios it's suddenly contending with. As the front door shuts behind him, I turn back to the empty coffee canister, frowning.

———

I'm still feeling nervous and uneasy when I sit down at my desk later that morning. And thanks to the lack of caffeine, I feel unprepared to take on my workday, which is only compounded when I see Brent has scheduled an impromptu meeting with me in twenty minutes. Whatever he wants to meet about can't be good. Whatever it is, it probably means more work is about to come my way. I eye the to-do list sitting next to my keyboard with a sigh, wishing I had done the smart thing this morning, and grabbed Nick's coffee right out of his hand. I figure I need it more than him. He's the one leaving the house, the one who can pick up his own coffee on the road.

The more I think about it, the more bitter I become, convinced Nick did it on purpose, that he's acting out on some long-buried resentment toward me. Punishment by caffeine withdrawal. Effective.

I manage to cross only one item off my list before Slack alerts me to a huddle from Brent. I click "Join," and Brent's face appears on the screen. I glance at the small window reflecting my face back to me, noting the stacks of books teetering precariously against the wall behind me. A flicker of annoyance takes root. Still no storage.

"Apologies for the last-minute call," Brent says. "I know you're busy, so I'll get right to it. I'm worried you're overstretched."

It takes every ounce of my willpower not to laugh, or to say, as Anna loves to say, "Duh!" Instead of answering, I just sit there, my eyes locked on his—or as close as you can come to locking eyes with someone over a computer screen. Even in the silence, I'm bothered by how calm he looks. I want to reach through the screen and pinch him, just to get a reaction.

Finally, I open my mouth to respond, but then it hits me—maybe it's the look in his eyes giving him away, I don't know, but I know he's not looking for validation. He wants me to tell him I'm fine, that everything's okay. And maybe the Colette of a few months ago would have assuaged his fears like I would an upset child, but I can't be that person anymore. If I want to save my sanity—and likely my marriage—I need to be more upfront and honest with my feelings.

"I *am* overstretched," I tell him in what I hope is an even tone. "And, before you say it, yes—I realize things are slipping through the cracks, which is what happens when a person can't handle their workload. I've been overstretched for months, even before Matt left, and, if you recall, I've already told you this once or twice."

For a brief moment, Brent looks as though I *have* reached through the screen and pinched him, but then he seems to catch himself. He clears his throat. "What can I do to help?"

I know from experience not to get too excited. *What can I do to help?* It's the same line he gave me last time and the time before. What I need is for him to go beyond just pretending to care about my well-being. What I need from him is the same thing I need at home from Nick, which is to feel appreciated and valued. Bosses who value their hard workers help them when they're overstretched. They don't make empty promises again and again.

Nick's words echo in my head. *I want you to be more open with me. I think you're keeping things too bottled up, and it makes them worse.*

I sit up straighter in my seat. "You have to find someone to replace Matt. It's been almost two months since he left and, while I did agree to take on his workload, it was only meant to be temporary. It's been nearly two months, and we're no closer to replacing him than we were when he left." I swallow, steeling myself. "You want to help me? That's easy. Find someone to manage the thriller imprint."

Brent no longer looks calm and collected. In fact, he looks as though he might finally be willing to take me seriously, which is to say his face is so flushed it reaches the tip of his ears.

The nerves, anger, and annoyance I felt before our call are gone, replaced with what I can only describe as a sense of triumph and accomplishment. I feel, for the first time in a long time, like a winner.

Life: 3, Colette: 4.

And there's only one person I can think of to share in my triumph.

———

It's easier than expected to find a reason to run into Zac. For example I know from our previous conversation over coffee that he's addicted to the house roast at Café Lola and has a bad habit of going there almost daily, which I find hilarious considering the vibe is clearly geared toward women—all pink couches and flower-covered walls; it's a millennial influencer's wildest dream come true. I also know he loves walking model homes, finding inspiration and comfort between their walls. I also learn, from a deep dive through various Instagram profiles—a winding, twisting, miles-long road to discovery—Zac's a Golden Knights fan and likes to catch their practices at City National Arena whenever he can. The latter piece of information doesn't help me seeing as we're fresh into the off-season, but I like knowing these tidbits about him I might not have known otherwise.

I drag the kids to Café Lola the following morning, where we sit drinking our overly sweet drinks for approximately an hour longer than either of them are happy with, and again the following Monday and Tuesday. It's on Wednesday, our fourth visit, that I finally get lucky.

Ben is the one who spots him first. A smile erupts across his face, and he jumps from his seat. "Zac!"

I wait exactly five seconds before I slowly lift my head, feigning surprise.

Zac closes the distance between us. "Hey guys, fancy seeing you here." He looks from the kids to me, smiling so brightly that the skin at the corner of his eyes wrinkles.

"Hi," I say—one word, only one syllable, and I give away my excitement.

I watch Zac register this, watch the corner of his mouth turn up even more. For years, I've chastised my authors for writing things like, *His eyes sparkled*, but now I know for a fact it actually happens…and when you least expect it. I'm transfixed, rooted to the spot, my eyes locked on his.

In the few moments we stand there locked in some sort of intimate bubble, my mind works double-time. In one breath, I'm back in my office crying, with his arm around me, and the next we're seated across from each other at the kitchen table drinking coffee. I'm stuck on the memory of discovering his eye color changes depending on the lighting, but it's when my gaze falls to his mouth that I finally snap to attention, the coffee shop reappearing around me.

Zac is still smiling, albeit timidly now. He looks toward the register and back again. "I'm going to go order a coffee. I'll..." He hesitates. "I'll be right back."

With him gone, I seem to come back to myself. Ben is happily chewing on his straw, staring off into space, but Anna's gaze is locked firmly on me.

"What even was that?" she asks.

"I have no idea what you're talking about."

She grimaces. "You're so embarrassing."

"Again, I have no idea what you're talking about."

Anna rolls her eyes and stands, reaching for Ben. "Come on, Ben. Let's go sit outside. Give Mom and Zac some space."

"Anna, don't be ridic—" I begin, but her palm stops me. I watch them head outside, my head swimming. An unsettling feeling forms in the pit of my stomach.

What the hell am I doing? I mean, seriously? I've already established my life is complicated as hell, that work is a pit of despair, my marriage is a mess, and my best friend seems intent on distancing herself forever, so why am I suddenly intent on making things even worse?

Zac is back at the table too quickly, a black coffee in hand —in a mug, not a to-go cup, indicating he intends to stay. I'm not surprised when he asks to join me, nor when my mouth is suddenly too dry to speak. We sit.

"How's the new banister holding up?" he asks. His face is lit up like a Christmas tree; a happy, satisfied, confident man.

I swallow past a lump in my throat. "It's great. What an improvement."

"And the storage issue? Has it been resolved?"

It's not his fault, really. He couldn't have known he just touched on a nerve. He couldn't have known what I would unleash on him. I have to think he wouldn't have asked the question if he had.

What comes out of my mouth isn't mean, but it isn't kind

either. I vent my frustrations with the house and the renovation and every little thing in between, my voice rising and falling in volume as I try to calm myself, to stop myself from going any further. It's verbal diarrhea in its worst form.

Finally, somehow, I manage to stop talking, but my heart is racing, and my hands shaking in a way I know has little to do with the caffeine I've ingested.

Zac exhales what sounds like a deep breath coupled with an awkward laugh, his eyebrows jumping.

"I'm sorry. God, I'm sorry. I don't know where that came from." Again, the memory of him consoling me in my office is with me. I drop my head into my hands. "I'm a total mess. You should go before I really lose my shit."

I bring myself to standing when his hand encircles my wrist. I look down at it, my heart still pounding in my chest. His hand is rough and calloused, dwarfing my own so much it's almost comical.

"Colette." His voice seems impossibly deep.

I wet my lips, unable to look at him. "Yeah?"

His response doesn't come right away. He seems to wait until I've gathered the strength to finally look at him again. "You are *phenomenal*."

I sink back down into my seat, feeling as though my insides have liquified. Dropping my voice to a whisper that can barely be heard over the buzz of chatter in the café, I say, "What did you just say?"

Zac's pale eyes lock on mine. "I said, you are phenomenal."

I press my eyes shut, wanting this moment to last forever while also needing it to end immediately. I can't be here like this with this man who is not my husband, thinking the thoughts I'm having.

Zac leans forward. I feel his hand brush mine. "Did you hear what I said? I—"

I stop him there. "Please. Don't say anything more. I—" I

take a shaky breath, feeling the sting of tears I'm desperate to avoid. "I should go."

I move quickly, unable and unwilling to look back. Once out the door, I wrangle the kids into the car, and I'm gone.

All this time, I've been silently judging Zoey for what she did to Aaron, putting myself up on a pedestal. I'm not perfect, but at least I wouldn't do that. I've thought this on numerous occasions.

Well, look at me now.

How easily we can all fall…

CHAPTER
TWENTY-THREE

By July, there is still no change in my workload, no sudden improvement in my children's behavior, nor is there any difference in Nick and my interactions. I still look like I haven't slept in years and am holding on to those twenty extra pounds for dear life. I somehow believed flying that close to the sun—the sun being Zac, of course—and not getting burned might shift things in my own universe. But every day I work my tail off until five p.m., only to then work my tail off at home until Nick deigns to come home from work. For the past two weeks, he's missed more dinners than not, and with no help from the kids no matter how much I bribe them, the house is beginning to resemble the one I grew up in with a slight sheen of dust on most every surface; the kind of home you wouldn't want to walk around barefoot in.

Around this time, a small bookshelf appears in my office, assembled and pushed against the back wall, parallel to my desk. I spend the first ten minutes of my workday filling it with my painstakingly alphabetized novels, but I barely reach "K" before I run out of space. I stack the rest of the books in a pile outside the shelf and settle into my desk for another day of torture. I don't think about the bookshelf, or where it came from. In fact, I push it out of my mind. If I don't, I might say something to Nick I'll regret. Something along the lines of a Band-Aid and a bullet hole.

———

Nick saunters in one night later that week, sometime between Ben slurping up his last mouthful of spaghetti and me pouring myself a second glass of wine—which, at just past five o'clock, isn't ideal. I'm angry and frustrated, performing the classic nighttime dance of the overburdened working mother. The wine is white and chilled and goes down smoothly. But, in hindsight, it's certainly not the best idea.

I send the kids upstairs to their rooms, ignoring their confused expressions. Normally, I'd do everything to reassure them, but I can't deal with their feelings right now. I'm not sure I'm even dealing well with my own.

Nick walks slowly to the sink, rinsing his coffee mug and dishes from lunch, looking unnaturally stiff. As I stare at his back, my chest tightens as all the guilt, anger, and resentment I've been feeling resurfaces.

My hand shakes as I set down my glass of wine. "Nick." My voice is shaky too.

He doesn't even turn around to face me. "Mm-hmm."

"Nick," I say again, more clearly this time.

This time he turns. I can pinpoint the moment he registers what's happening—the look on my face, my body language, the way I seem to be breathing erratically. He steps toward me. "What is it?"

I have to say it before I lose my nerve. "This isn't working."

Nick frowns. "What isn't?"

"This," I say. "How things are."

He stands perfectly still and silent, which only serves to fan the flame of my anger.

"'I see what you're doing,'" I say. "'I wanted you to know.' Those were your exact words to me. I pulled back on my work hours so I could have more time for the kids, more time for this family. And what did you do? You took that as permission to increase your work hours, to increase your time away from the family—with no discussion about how I might feel.

"If you *had* told me what you were thinking, we could have avoided all this. We could have avoided making things even harder between us. But once again, my feelings aren't being taken into consideration."

I reach for my wine glass, nearly knocking it over in the process. One large sip and half the glass is gone. Nick watches me, his expression unreadable. I keep waiting for him to speak, but he seems at war with himself and his thoughts.

Eventually, I recognize the silence for what it truly is—a grown man's temper tantrum.

My words are venom. "Grow the fuck up."

Upstairs, I stand over the bathroom sink, viciously wiping the makeup from my face with a damp cloth. The wine has left me feeling dizzy.

Nick appears next to me. I hadn't been certain he would follow me. "Nothing I do pleases you, do you know that? No matter how much time I spend with the kids, how much money I make, how much money I spend, how many hours I work. I can't ever get it right. I was home by five tonight. Five." His eyes are wild with anger as he stares at my reflection in the mirror. "Why don't you tell me what you want me to do? You can write up a schedule for me, tell me where you want me and when."

I stop washing my face and turn to him. "I already have two kids; I don't need a third. When you're willing to have an adult conversation, let me know." I dry my face and leave the bathroom, turning off the light behind me.

Nick follows. "You wanted to have this conversation, Letty, so let's have it. You say things aren't working the way they are, so tell me what you want me to do. Tell me what will finally make you happy. Tell me—"

"I wanted to leave!" The tone of my voice alarms even me. "I didn't want to stay here. I didn't want to renovate; I wanted to move into the housing tract I showed you. But I listened to that voice in the back of my head, the one reminding me I'm always running away when things aren't perfect. I don't want to continue being that person. You wanted to stay and make it work, and so I decided I wanted it too."

Nick exhales. "I gave you everything you wanted. Everything on the list you wrote. I—"

"Storage, Nick! We need storage. Yes, I have a beautifully renovated kitchen and an office I desperately needed, and our banister doesn't shake under our hands anymore, but we still don't have enough room to store our belongings properly. We're still bursting at the seams. And I just can't figure out how we ended up here, how it wasn't clear that more storage was nonnegotiable." I pinch my eyes shut as the room sways slightly. Lowering myself slowly onto the edge of the bed, I say, "You told me to trust you, Nick. You told me to trust it would all work out."

"I thought it would all work out," he says. I expect more anger, but his tone is one of defeat. "I knew you wanted to move, but I didn't. I still don't. As for the renovations, I had a plan for everything, but I couldn't figure out how to create more storage out of thin air. I worked on giving you everything else you asked for, thinking the solution to the storage problem would somehow present itself along the way."

"This is your job, Nick, what you're literally paid to do every day, and you're trying to tell me you—what—expected to magically find extra space where there is none?" I shake my head. "I can't believe you."

"We'll figure something out."

"How?" I massage my temples.

He has no answer, of course.

"You wanted me to be more open with you, so here I am. I'm pissed off, Nick. I'm angry we went through the mess of renovations without solving one of our biggest problems. I'm angry you didn't take me seriously. I'm annoyed that you thought assembling a tiny bookshelf in my office would solve anything." He tries to speak, but I stop him. "Most of all, I'm pissed that you're trying to turn this around on me and make this about me being hard to please. Because that's bullshit."

I stand up from the bed, ignoring the headache already forming. "All this time I thought I had figured out what our problems are, but I'm realizing now we've only scratched the surface. Our issues run a lot deeper than I thought." I turn and settle my eyes on him. "I've done enough obsessing over the problems in our marriage this year. How about you take over for a while."

In the closet, I pull down an overnight bag and start filling it with t-shirts, underwear, bras, and a few pairs of jeans. In the bathroom, I gather my makeup, skincare, and toothbrush.

Nick pauses in the doorway. "What's happening here?"

I scoff. "What does it look like, Nick?"

He doesn't move from his spot as I continue pushing items into the overnight bag. I'm not entirely sure what's happening, but whatever it is, it feels right. It feels necessary.

I leave the bag at the top of the stairs and go to see the kids. I kiss Ben, who's playing with LEGOs, twice on the temple and tell him I love him. Anna is on her phone when I enter her room through her open door. She looks anything but enthused when I tell her I love her, but she allows me to press my lips to her temple.

I walk past Nick, still standing in the bedroom doorway, watching me, and carry my bag downstairs. It's not until I have my car keys in hand that he finally speaks.

"Where are you going?"

I pause by the front door, my right palm pressed flat against its surface. I speak slowly, and calmly. "It's like I said, Nick, I'm done obsessing over the problems in our marriage this year. It's your turn."

I open the door and step through it. "You take care of the kids, the cooking, and all the other hundred things I do for this family every day." I turn to face him. "I'll come back when I'm ready."

I'd told him. I absorb it all, I'd said.

CHAPTER
TWENTY-FOUR

I drive north, unsure of where I'm going, my earlier wine buzz fading the moment I step out of the house. With each mile I put between myself and home, my mind feels sharper and clearer. The motion settles my thoughts, the hum of tires on the road making everything seem less tangled, less impossible.

I need a break from my life, I think, repeating it like a mantra as the city lights blur by in my peripheral vision. The houses and storefronts, the strip malls and streetlights—they all pass in a soft haze. I need a break from *everything*—the house, the kids, Nick, the endless to-do list that never seems to get any shorter. What I need most is sleep, real, deep sleep, the kind you only have before you have kids, before your entire life becomes a constant state of alertness, waiting for the next problem, the next thing you forgot to do.

Sleep, and time. Time to think. Time to decide what I want my life to look like moving forward, what I'm simply tolerating, and what I'm pretending doesn't bother me. Time to face the reality I've been shoving down for years now.

When I pull up outside the model home, I'm not surprised.

I've always been drawn here, to this image of perfection, this fantasy life existing behind four pristine walls. It's always felt like a symbol of hope—a promise of a fresh start if I just dared to take it.

It's late—too late to be here, really—but when the saleswoman waves me in, I don't hesitate. I step through the front doors and into the foyer, past the small den and into the great room, where I stop. I take a deep breath, letting the quiet wash over me. Already, I can feel my thoughts falling into place, as if the silence of this empty, perfect house is giving me the clarity I've been desperate for.

I move through the kitchen, letting my fingers trail across the countertops, cold and smooth beneath my skin. I stop between the island and the sink and close my eyes. I can almost see it—me, standing here, dicing tomatoes for a salad, chicken parmesan in the oven, the smell of cheese and basil filling the air. The kids are at the table, finishing their homework, their stomachs growling. There's a bottle of white wine chilling in the fridge—a housewarming gift from a friend, one I'll share with Zoey, once we patch things up.

But when my eyes drift to the head of the table where Nick usually sits, the chair is empty.

I pull myself away from the kitchen, moving down the hallway toward the bedrooms, the fantasy unraveling as I go. Anna and Ben would be fighting over the bigger room, Anna insisting she deserves it because she's older, and Ben demanding it because it's closer to the bathroom. I would have to step in, like I always do, referee their bickering, and settle things in a way that leaves everyone just a little bit unhappy.

Even in the perfect house, nothing is truly perfect.

In the master bedroom, I picture Nick—lying in bed, his arm thrown over his head the way he sleeps, a soft snore escaping his lips. The sight of him there, so familiar and yet so far away, makes my chest ache. How did we get here? How did I get here? When did everything become so tangled, so impossible?

Suddenly, I can't stand being in this fantasy anymore. I move quickly through the house, my feet heavy on the floor, my pulse loud in my ears. I make it back to the great room, sink down onto the couch, and bury my face in my hands. The tears come before I can stop them.

I've been holding everything together for so long, and now, sitting here, alone, I realize just how tired I am. How broken. How lost.

My phone buzzes in my purse, and I pull it out to see Nick's name on the screen.

I'm sorry.

The words blur through my tears, but I can't bring myself to reply. What is he sorry for? For not listening when I said I couldn't handle everything on my own? For making me feel invisible? For letting our marriage fall apart?

I toss the phone back in my purse, my thoughts spiraling. We're in serious trouble, and an apology isn't going to fix it. I'm not even sure if we *can* fix it.

As I drive aimlessly, the tension in my chest builds, my thoughts racing faster than the passing streetlights. This isn't just about Nick, I realize. It's about me. I don't know who I am anymore. I've been the wife, the mother, the fixer—but I don't know what *I* want. I don't know if I even want to stay in this life.

A gas station appears on my right, and without thinking, I jerk the wheel hard and pull into the parking lot. My heart is pounding in my ears. I sit in the car for a few seconds, then step out, slamming the door behind me. I march across the lot, feeling a strange rush of adrenaline, the same kind I felt years ago when I made reckless decisions just because I could.

I walk into the building, my mind buzzing with half-formed thoughts, and grab a pack of cigarettes. I haven't smoked in years, but right now, it feels like the only thing that makes sense.

The cashier barely looks up as he rings me up, and I don't even care. My hands shake as I pull out cash to pay, feeling a strange mix of guilt and exhilaration as I walk out, the pack of cigarettes burning a hole in my pocket.

Outside, I lean against the car, tear open the pack, and light one up. I inhale deeply, the familiar burn in my lungs bringing back a flood of memories. I quit smoking when I got pregnant with Anna, and I haven't touched a cigarette since. But right now, the smoke feels like rebellion—like I'm doing something just for me, something bad for me, something I can control.

I take another drag, feeling the tension in my body loosen slightly. It's stupid. It's reckless. But it's something *I* chose. Something that has nothing to do with Nick, or the kids, or the house.

But as I stand there, the cigarette burning down between my fingers, the guilt creeps back in. I haven't done something this impulsive in years. I know Nick would hate this. Hell, I hate it. But I needed it. I needed to feel like I had control over *something* in my life, even if it's just a stupid cigarette.

I finish the cigarette, toss it to the ground, and grind it under my heel. The momentary rush fades, and I feel the weight of everything settle back on my shoulders. What am I doing? This isn't going to solve anything.

I slide back into the car, the smell of smoke clinging to my hair and clothes, and drive until I end up at a dingy two-star hotel by the library. It's the kind of place no one notices, where you can disappear for a while without anyone caring. It's perfect.

For the next two days, I hide. I avoid Nick's texts, ignore calls from the office, and bury myself in work I don't care about. I eat greasy takeout, drink bad hotel coffee, and spend too much time watching terrible reality TV shows. It's mindless, but it's what I need right now.

My phone lights up with messages from Nick.

> What time is camp pickup?
> What does Ben like for lunch? He won't tell me.
> Did you know Anna's been wearing makeup?

I stare at the messages, my chest tight. Part of me wants to answer him, to give him the information he's asking for. But another part of me—the part that's still standing outside the gas station with a cigarette between my fingers—wants to let him figure it out on his own.

I close the messages and toss the phone onto the bed. I'm not ready to go back. I'm not ready to deal with all the things waiting for me at home.

I let myself imagine—*What if this were my life?* What if I could stay here, in this dingy hotel, with no one to answer to? What if I could wake up whenever I wanted, make breakfast just for myself, leave the house whenever I felt like it? What if I didn't have to deal with Nick's silence, or Anna's teenage attitude, or Ben's constant need for attention?

What if it were just me?

The fantasy is tempting. But deep down, I know it's just that—a fantasy. I'm a mother. I'm a wife. There's no going back, no matter how much I want to escape it sometimes.

I sigh and get up, pacing the room. I'm not spiraling, but I'm not sure what I'm doing either. I feel numb. Empty. Lost.

And yet, for the first time in years, I'm not overthinking every decision. I'm just *existing*.

I shake my head, forcing the thoughts away. I know I'll have to go back. I know I can't avoid my life forever. But for now, I need this. One more night. One more day.

I pull out my phone again and scroll through the messages from Nick. I type a reply, then delete it. I don't know what to say. I don't even know how to begin fixing what's broken between us.

So instead, I grab the remote, turn on the TV, and let the mindless chatter of bad reality shows fill the silence. One more day. One more night.

I'll figure it out tomorrow.

CHAPTER
TWENTY-FIVE

When I first left, my thoughts were surprisingly helpful, even productive. Maybe Anna and I just need more one-on-one time to fix things. Maybe it's not as complicated as it feels— just reconnecting over simple moments like we used to. Could initiating sex really be as simple as they say? Fake it 'til you make it? I smiled at the idea, almost amused. And the kids —this time with just their dad—maybe it was exactly what they needed. Maybe it was special for them. For him.

I let myself believe that for a while, let it feel like a reprieve, like I'd made the right decision to step away.

But eventually, those positive thoughts fade, giving way to something darker, something more bitter. I start picturing Nick struggling to keep up with the day-to-day chaos— scrambling to make five days' worth of meals, dealing with the endless stream of questions from the kids, each one more impossible to answer than the last. *How many times has he heard Ben call for "Dad" and wished I were there instead? How many mornings has he had to beg Ben to brush his teeth, plead with him to get out of bed, make his lunch, eat his breakfast, all while running late for work? How is he possibly managing to juggle it all?* I bet he's exhausted.

Good, a petty part of me whispers. *Let him see what it's like.*

For five days, he's been living my life, stepping into my daily existence—the relentless routine that's ground me down. He's felt the weight of it all, the endless balancing act, the exhaustion no sleep can cure. I bet he's falling into bed every night, completely drained, just like I always have.

Why don't you tell me what you want me to do? You can write up a schedule for me, tell me where you want me and when, he'd said, as if my life could be managed by a spreadsheet.

Well, now he's exactly where I've wanted him—home with our family, *present.* Except it's not because he wants to be. It's because he has no other choice. He's filling in the gaps because I left them wide open.

And here I am, the one disappearing. The one who ran.

I try to tell myself this is what I need—a break, some space to breathe. But the truth presses against my chest like a weight I can't escape. I'm the one who left. I'm the one running from my problems, just like I always do. Why is it easier for me to stand up to Brent at work, to demand what I need there, but so impossibly hard in my own marriage?

My thoughts spin faster, louder. There's a stack of pillows next to me, and I grab one, pulling it over my face, pressing it tightly against my ears to block out the noise in my head. Everything goes dark, blessedly silent, the world muffled behind the soft weight of the pillow. I squeeze my eyes shut, desperate for the silence to last.

Sometime later, I wake up, disoriented. The pillow is still half-draped over my face, the sheets tangled around my legs, sticky with sweat. I push the comforter off with my feet, trying to shake the grogginess. The room is stifling, and it takes me a moment to remember where I am. The puke-colored blinds, the worn carpet. It's nearly ten, and I've slept for seven hours straight.

I sit up slowly, wiping at my eyes, my head still heavy with sleep. I reach for my phone, my fingers fumbling as I dig around for it under the pillow next to me. When I finally unlock it, my thumb hovers over the Messages app. Over Nick's name.

I don't know what to say. I don't know what I *can* say. I've spent the last few months telling him how I feel, explaining what I need, and none of it has changed anything. I've given him the roadmap—everything he needs to make things better—and still, here we are.

I'd told him as I walked out the door, that it was his turn to obsess over the state of our marriage, to worry about us the way I've been worrying for years. And I meant it. I've been holding everything together for so long. It's his turn to step up, to fight for us.

Except—

I push myself into a sitting position, the sheets pooling around my waist as I stare at the screen.

I miss him.

The realization hits me with such force I nearly drop the phone. I miss him. I miss him so much, so suddenly, the weight of it almost knocks me back down. I don't just miss him in some vague, nostalgic way—I miss him in a deep, desperate way, in the way you miss something that's been a part of you for so long you didn't even realize it until it was gone.

I miss the small moments—the feel of his arm brushing against mine in bed, the way he absently runs a hand through my hair when he's half-asleep, the sound of his laughter when he's with the kids. I miss the comfort of him being there, even when we're disconnected, even when things aren't right.

And that's when I know. I need to go home. I need to go

back, no matter how hard it's going to be. No matter how much work is waiting for us. Running away isn't the solution. This break, this distance, it's only shown me how nothing will change unless I go back and do the work alongside him.

Still, there's a part of me that resists. A small, rebellious part doesn't want to let go of this fleeting freedom, this tiny slice of independence I've carved out for myself.

I glance at the clock—10:10 p.m. The night is warm, sticky, and thick. No one's around. I head outside, slipping into the shadowy parking lot. I walk aimlessly, letting my feet lead me away from the hotel, past the dimly lit storefronts, until I find myself in front of a 24-hour diner. Without thinking, I step inside, the cool air-conditioning a stark contrast to the heat outside. The place is nearly empty, save for a tired waitress behind the counter and an old man nursing a cup of coffee in the corner. I slide into a booth and pick up the sticky laminated menu, the options blurring together in the fluorescent light.

I order a milkshake. Something indulgent, something I don't need but desperately want. The cold sweetness coats my throat, grounding me in the present, in this tiny act of rebellion. For a moment, I let myself imagine a different life. A life where this is my normal, where I don't have a husband waiting for me at home, where I don't have kids who rely on me for everything. A life where I can be as selfish as I want, where I only have to think about myself.

But the fantasy is fleeting. The last sip of the milkshake disappears, and with it, the illusion of escape. The reality is I do have a husband waiting for me. I have a family that needs me. And I want them. Despite everything—the frustration, the exhaustion, the resentment—I want them.

And I want to fix this.

I leave a few crumpled bills on the table, pushing away the

empty glass, and take a deep breath. I'll go home. But I'll be damned if I let Nick know how close I came to running.

I slip back into the hotel, kicking off my shoes and grabbing the travel-size bottle of body spray from my bag. I scrub my skin raw in the shower, rinsing away the sticky heat of the night, the taste of something forbidden, the last remnants of my little rebellion. By the time I'm done, I feel lighter.

I'll go home. I'll face Nick, the kids, the house. But more than that—I'll do the work. I won't just show up. I'll fight for us, for our family, for me.

———

The house is dark as I round the corner and pull into the garage. Inside, it's so quiet it feels as though I've somehow entered the wrong house by mistake. But there in the hallway are Ben's favorite flip-flops, worn and misshapen from overuse, and on the narrow hall table, Nick's clipboard, stacked with notes and invoices. I know if I flip it over, I'll see two stickers: one featuring his company logo and the other a small image of Grogu Ben stuck on there one morning when he was up before everyone else, bored and looking for something to do. I touch the papers with my fingers, almost like I don't think they're real, and then, after glancing up the dark stairwell, I take a deep breath and climb the stairs.

I'm not surprised to find Nick asleep, not after these days spent living my reality. I watch him for a moment, willing him awake, but he keeps sleeping.

Instead of getting into bed, I take my wide-awake self and a glass of wine outside to the backyard, where I sweat through my clothes almost immediately, the desert summer heat relentless even at night. But still, I sit. I try to think of what I would tell Nick if he wakes up, but my thoughts are jumbled.

As I look out at the palm trees and across the yard to the

small pool, an immense sadness spreads through me. As necessary as it feels to fix my relationship with Nick, there's still an ache in my heart from missing Zoey. I'm not sure how I'm going to mend my marriage, but beyond that, I feel completely lost when it comes to getting my best friend back. It seems with every week that passes, it'll be harder to find our way back to each other. Every day she's without me, she could be finding it easier to stay away.

"Mom?" Anna's voice startles me.

I turn to face her as she rubs her eyes and adjusts the over-sized t-shirt she wears to sleep.

"Hi, Banana." I reach for her, and she comes, sitting down beside me. "Can't sleep?"

"I didn't know when you were coming home."

I sigh. How can I explain it to her, this person of mine who's not yet a woman but beyond just a girl? "I know, and I'm sorry. Please know it wasn't something you or your brother did. I just really needed some time to myself."

Anna's head drops onto my shoulder, and I hold my body still as can be, so as not to scare her off. "I get it. Sometimes I need some space, too."

I press my lips to the top of her head, never wanting to move. My girl, my beautiful, smart girl. Here she is, healthy and thriving—doing exactly what girls her age are meant to do, even if I don't like it. "I'm home now," I say. "I'm not going anywhere."

What was it I'd been so scared of? Anna isn't doing anything wrong; she's doing just what she's meant to do—growing up, developing autonomy and independence. There's nothing wrong with her. It's my way of thinking that's the problem.

Change is the only constant.

I can't force Anna to open up to me; I can only be aware enough to enjoy the moments when she does. And I can't make Nick into someone he's not, just as I can't suddenly be someone I'm not. We need to be better for each other...*to* each other. That's all there is to it. Somewhere along the line, I forgot to look at all the blessings I've been granted. I forgot what Zoey told me long ago: the grass is greener where you water it.

It's not too late to turn my marriage around or to fix what's broken with Zoey. I might not have all the answers, but I know I have to keep trying.

————

Nick doesn't stir as I ready myself for bed, nor does he move an inch when I get into bed next to him. I sit there for an hour, unable to sleep, unable to quiet my mind. But still, he sleeps. Eventually, I turn off the light and lie down, arranging and rearranging myself until I find a comfortable position. Behind my lids, I feel myself relax until finally, I, too, fall asleep.

When I open my eyes again, Nick is watching me, his stale breath filling the space between us. "You're home."

The room is dark, and the clock next to me reads 4:05.

I leap into Nick's arms, attaching myself to him.

"I'm glad you're home," he whispers.

Tears prick my eyes. I blink, wishing them away. There's so much I need to say to him, but the words are jumbled inside my mouth, unable to come out.

All I can do is cry.

CHAPTER
TWENTY-SIX

I wake up three hours later, anxious to begin my day. I press a kiss against Nick and slip on my housecoat, heading downstairs to prepare breakfast. I decide to make blueberry buttermilk pancakes—a recipe of my mother's—because I'm in the mood for them, but the kids are thrilled nonetheless. I have the urge to ask what they ate while I was away, but I think better of it. Bygones and all that.

Along with the pancakes, I make a pot of coffee I'll drink over the next few hours, set Ben up at the table with a canvas and some discount paint I picked up a couple of weeks ago, and head back upstairs to shower and get dressed.

An hour later, at my desk, I glance over my email, assessing the importance of each message. Once I decide nothing is requiring my immediate attention, I pick up my cell phone and dial the number I've been wanting to for months.

"Hi." Zoey's voice on the other end of the line feels like a breath of fresh air.

"Zoey. Hi," I breathe. "I—I didn't expect you to answer."

"I'm kind of surprised myself."

Now that I have her on the line, I don't know where to start. "Hi," I say again. My mind is whirling, my thoughts tripping over one another. I want to ask why she shut me out, and why she hasn't returned my calls. I want to know how someone could treat their best friend this way. I'm desperate to know how she is, how the twins and Aaron are doing. I have no idea what's going on in her life, and it's killing me.

"Zoey, I—" I hesitate. "Is everything okay?"

"Not really, but it will be."

I try to stay calm, but I'm just so happy she answered my call. "I've been worried about you. I know you told me to stay in my own lane, but you're my best friend, and I'm going to worry about you, especially if I don't hear from you for—"

"Stop."

I clamp my mouth shut. Zoey is quiet on the other end of the line. I wait for her to speak, sure that what she says next will explain away her silence these past months. Whatever it is, I'm ready to move past it and get back to the way things used to be.

Instead, she says, "I have to go."

And she does.

———

The kids and I finish dinner and clean up by the time Nick arrives home from work. I feel the familiar tug of annoyance build inside me the moment he comes through the door, but then, like a giddy teenager, he produces a bouquet of peonies from behind his back. I feel equally giddy as I push my face into them, inhaling their sweet floral scent.

"I realized it's been too long since I bought you flowers."

It's one of those tiny things that time, comfort, and predictability have taken from our marriage.

As I put the flowers into a vase and fill it with water, he

moves around me, tidying up what's left from dinner. There isn't much since I cleaned as I cooked, and soon, Nick turns to me, pressing his back against the countertop. I know immediately I'm not going to like what he has to say. Maybe it's the way he can't quite look me in the eye that gives away his intentions, or maybe it's just that, after all these years, I know when he's about to give me bad news.

"Do you have a moment? Can we sit?"

I set the flowers on the table and take a seat in front of them, feeling suddenly silly now I know the true intentions behind him giving them to me. Nick walks around the table and sits opposite me, clasping his hands in front of him.

"You were right, what you said the other day…about me taking on more work recently." He pulls in a shaky breath, and I lean in closer. "I didn't talk it over with you because I hadn't really thought it through. All I knew was more jobs meant bringing in more money, and that seemed like the smart thing to do. A lot of the guys I'm working with could really benefit from the extra hours, and, well, I thought it couldn't hurt us either. I knew you'd be upset about the renovations not solving all our problems, and you'd add it to the long list of things you're unhappy with me about." Here, he pauses. I stay silent, my thoughts stuck on how he's twisted things to make me look like the bad guy again. He continues: "I know now I was avoiding you, avoiding being home because I thought it might be easier this way. I guess I thought a little more space might do us some good, but I see now how wrong I was to make those decisions without consulting you first. And I'm sorry."

I look to the peonies, then back at Nick, and say, "Thank you for telling me."

Nick's eyes search mine. He, too, is looking for answers to questions he doesn't want to ask. "My hours are going to continue to be hectic for a while as we start the new projects we signed on for, but I'll do what I can to help you whenever possible."

"I get it," I say. And I do. He's made promises he needs to follow through on. I won't hold it against him. It's a good thing his business is successful, that he's able to stay so busy. He's supporting his family just like I am with my work. In fact, he's never once complained about me working too hard, and has never made me feel less than for being a hard worker, the way I've done to him.

The plan comes to me, fully formed. All I have to do is be brave enough to enact it.

———

I wait until late Friday afternoon to request a last-minute meeting with Brent. When he appears on my screen, tall glass of beer in hand and ready for the long weekend, I know I've chosen the right time.

"Colette," he says. "What can I do for you?"

I don't need to take a deep breath or build myself up—I'm ready.

"I wanted to circle back to the discussion we had about me being overstretched."

"Okay."

"Have you made any progress in finding someone to handle the thriller imprint?"

He sets down his drink. "I've got my feelers out, but it hasn't been long since we last discussed it. It's going to take ti—"

"I think I'm out of time, Brent."

"What do you mean?"

I close my eyes for a moment, willing myself to slow down. When I open them again, he's staring at me, his earlier calm demeanor replaced with something else entirely. "I've been a great employee, and I know you'd agree. I've been doing the job of more than one person for years, which is why you wouldn't want to lose me and be in an even bigger hole than you are now. Brent—" I speak as calmly as possible, "In order to keep being a great employee, I need to cut back my hours."

Brent is still. "That's not possible."

I smile sadly. "I'm afraid it's going to have to be. I've given you everything I have for over ten years now, sometimes to the detriment of my own family. But I'm telling you I need to cut back my hours by at least twenty-five percent, though I'd prefer to go straight part-time."

"I don't know what to say. I don't know how that would work."

"I love my job, you know I do, but I'm not going to put it above my family. What I need right now is to focus on them, and to do so I need to work much less. It won't be permanent, it's just what I need right now."

Brent's mouth is a firm straight line. "When are you looking to make the transition?" he asks.

"I'm going to talk it over with my husband, but I think I can give you another three to four weeks. My kids go back to school on August fifteenth. I'll need to have transitioned to part-time by then."

"This is a big ask," he says.

Now I take a deep breath. "I understand if it doesn't work for you, and if so, I'll give you my notice now, but I hope it doesn't come to that."

"I'll need you to help me find someone to cover you," he says.

"I've always told you I'm here to help in any way I can."

As soon as the call ends, I sink back into my chair, relief flooding over me. Then I reach for my phone and send a message to Nick: *I have something I'd like to talk to you about tonight.* I follow it up with a happy face emoji so he knows it's nothing to worry about.

———

"So, what do you think?" I'm looking down at Mayer curled up in my lap as I say it.

Nick sighs—though it doesn't sound like one born of frustration or anger or even disappointment. It just is. "How long have you been thinking about wanting to cut back your hours?"

"Is that… Does that matter?"

"Not really," he says. "The timing just seems…"

I feel just a hint of hostility in the air. "I think what you're asking is whether or not I'd been thinking about cutting back before you told me you've taken on more work, and the answer is no." Being the baby I am, I continue to avoid making eye contact. "But yes, the timing is…convenient. It feels kismet."

"Kismet," he repeats.

I stroke Mayer softly as I say, "Did I ever tell you Zoey's theory about what my biggest problem is?" He shakes his head, so I continue. "She told me, probably years ago, that I'm stuck in the past, trying to exist in a time before kids and everything."

"Hmm."

I make a face.

He's been pacing the room and finally comes to a stop. "Well, what did you want me to say?"

I don't have an answer—not a good one anyway. The truth is, I hadn't given Zoey's comment much thought when she first said it—granted, she'd been using it as a jumping-off point to explain why my sex life had fallen off track. But it's one of those memories that came back to me during my sabbatical the previous week, and I've been questioning the truth behind her words ever since. She told me I needed to think outside the box more. I guess I'm trying to do just that.

Mayer jumps off my lap as Nick approaches me.

"I guess I'm just curious what the end game is?"

In an ideal world, my working less would result in increased happiness all around: I could focus on the kids, and rebuild the foundation beneath Nick and my marriage, and Brent, without his safety net, would finally do the right thing and get me some real help. And I could finally sort things out with Zoey. Everything could go back to the way it should be.

"Happiness," I say. "Satisfaction. That's always the end game." I reach for Nick's hands and urge him to sit down next to me. "I've been thinking a lot about what I want to do to take care of me, to take care of this family. There's so much we don't have control of in this life. I just want to be the best version of myself I can be—the best mother, wife, and person I can be. I want to be able to look back on my life and be proud of the work I've done, the beautiful children we created, the relationships I have."

Nick smiles softly.

"I want to look back on my life and feel full," I say. "Fullness, Nick."

"And you feel you need to—and I don't mean anything by this, I'm just truly curious—cut back on your work hours to…" He stumbles over his words.

"In order to fix things, yes."

He nods once, slowly. "Okay, okay, I understand."

I go back to my earlier question. "So, what do you think?"

He squeezes my hand. I've almost forgotten he's holding it. "I think, when it comes to this family, you know best. And maybe I haven't been so great at showing that, but I'm trying."

Maybe it's the sincerity I see in his eyes or the fact we've already been so vulnerable with each other, but I know there's more needing to be said.

"I wanted to talk about me walking out last week," I say. "I'm not sorry for taking the time to myself I desperately needed. I stand by my decision and I'd do it again. But I am sorry for how I went about it. I let my annoyance with everything get the best of me. I shouldn't have left like that."

Nick's body seems to relax. I feel it as well as see it.

"Thank you," he says.

I wait, perhaps stupidly, for an apology that, as the silence grows and grows, clearly isn't coming. The hope and peace I felt just a moment ago fizzles, replaced by a growing tightness in my chest.

I stand quickly, surprising him. I find myself pacing the bedroom.

"What's happening?" he says.

"'Thank you'?" I repeat. "Is that all you have to say?"

Nick looks confused, which only flares my anger.

"How about 'I'm sorry too, Colette'? I'm sorry for what I said and did too."

He's quiet, and I can't help but wonder if he's trying to go back to that night and remember what he said, what I think he deserves to apologize for. Just when I think I'm going to have to rehash everything word for word, he seems to come back to life.

"Are we still talking about the remodel?"

I throw my hands up in the air.

"So…yes?" He stands, shaking his head. "Sell the house then, Letty. Do what you want if you're so miserable here."

I know women who would have stopped talking then. Women who, having successfully gotten what they'd set out for, would move on, happy to have gotten their way, even if it had come about all wrong. I was that woman once, but I won't make the same mistake again.

"Don't do that," I say.

"It's what you wanted all along, isn't it? We'll sell the house you didn't want anymore anyway, and we'll move into the housing tract you love so much. Whatever it takes for me to stop having to hear about how I didn't give you what you needed."

"You wanted me to be more open with you."

He pinches his mouth shut, his lips turning white. "Yeah, yeah, I did." He nods curtly. "Fat lot of good it's done for us."

"The only way out is through," I say, though it's not entirely helpful.

Nick grunts. "Cute."

"I'm serious though, Nick. Our marriage isn't going to magically improve just because you admitted you want me to initiate sex more, or told me I need a hobby to get me out of the house. And while you've made some progress on my requests, there's still a lot of work to be done."

"Oh, believe me, I know." He pinches his eyes shut. "Just tell me what you want from me, Letty. I'm exhausted."

Through some divine miracle, I stop myself from saying, *Welcome to my life*. Nick and I are sitting on a precipice now. What we do next could have a monumental impact on the rest of our lives.

My gaze lingers on the nightstand.

The grass is greener where you water it.

Before I can change my mind or lose my nerve, I move to the nightstand, digging around for a moment before I find what I'm searching for.

"You want to know what I want from you? Why I'm so exhausted? Here you go." I throw the pad of paper at him, watching as it lands at his feet. He bends down to pick it up. I memorized what it says long ago, and I watch him read it, knowing exactly what he's seeing, line for line.

INVENTORY OF OUR MARITAL PROBLEMS

1. I have to take care of almost everything at home despite both of us working FT
2. No romance, little sex
3. I don't feel appreciated—when was the last time I heard 'thank you?'
4. He knows little about the day-to-day details of what's going on in the kids' lives
5. He has to be taught basic life skills—loading the dishwasher, laundry
6. He gives me the silent treatment when he's mad
7. He micromanages the budget/makes me feel bad about spending
8. I always have to be the bad guy when it comes to parenting (because I'm home more)
9. He doesn't consider my feelings
10. He has a hard time considering things from others' perspectives
11. We've stopped trying to look good for one another
12. Passive versus active—always waits for me to tell him what needs to be done (I'm not his mother!)
13. We're not talking like we used to

"I know that was probably difficult to read, and I'm sorry." Tears form in my eyes. "But I—"

"I've read it before," he says. He doesn't sound angry, or sad, or anything really. Stoic. It's the word that eventually comes to mind—he's stoic as he sits on the edge of the bed, staring back at me.

CHAPTER
TWENTY-SEVEN

For sixteen long seconds, Nick stares at me. I know because I count every single one of them, as fear and doubt take root, burrowing deep into my chest. My heart pounds in my ears, and I can't tell if it's from shock or dread. Did he really just say, *I've read it before*, or have I finally lost my mind?

I open my mouth to speak, but nothing comes out. The silence between us is suffocating, thick with all the words neither of us has dared to say out loud. I want to ask him to repeat himself, but I'm afraid I already know the answer. The disbelief still pulses through me, a dull ache.

Eventually, I manage to choke out something, maybe, "What?" or "Pardon?" though it probably sounds more like a garbled, "Excuse me?" Whatever it is, it's weak, and certainly not enough to untangle the mess between us now.

Nick lets out a slow, deliberate sigh, setting the pad of paper down gently on the bed beside him like it's something fragile, something that could shatter at any moment if handled too roughly. Without breaking eye contact, he moves closer to me. Step by step, at an excruciatingly slow pace, until we're so close our noses nearly touch. I can feel the heat of his body, the tension vibrating between us.

"I found your list," he says again, this time the words more measured, precise, like he's afraid they'll detonate if he's not careful with them.

I feel my stomach drop, like I've missed a step on a staircase, the sickening realization hitting me all at once. This isn't a misunderstanding. He's known—*he's known for months*.

"W-when?" I ask, my voice barely a whisper. I already know the answer, but I need to hear him say it. I need confirmation of this new reality.

Nick's jaw tightens, and he runs a hand through his hair, his eyes never leaving mine. "The night we went to Trattoria Reggiano," he says quietly, the words hanging in the air between us like a ticking time bomb.

I blink, trying to remember the night he's referring to. My mind races, trying to fit the pieces together. "That was… back in May," I say slowly, piecing it together. "As in—"

"Three months ago, yes."

Three months. I stagger back a step, the weight of his words hitting me like a physical blow. He's known about the list for three whole months, and I had no idea. He's been carrying this knowledge around with him, while I've been walking around blissfully ignorant, still believing I had time to figure everything out. He's been keeping this secret while I've been silently falling apart.

"You've known about the list for three months?" My voice comes out sharper than I intend, tinged with disbelief and something darker—something like betrayal.

Nick's eyes flash with a mixture of hurt and anger, and for a moment, I wonder if I've pushed him too far. But then he exhales, shaking his head slightly. "I've known for three months you've been keeping a record of every single thing you hate about me," he says, his voice low and controlled. "I've known that instead of talking to me, instead of letting me in, you've been writing down everything wrong in our marriage like it's some sort of inventory of all my failures."

I feel a hot flush of shame spread across my cheeks and my first instinct is to defend myself. To tell him it's not what he thinks, the list wasn't meant to hurt him, and it was just my way of organizing my thoughts. But the truth is, that's exactly what it was. I wrote the list in a moment of anger, a moment when I felt completely overwhelmed by everything —by him, by the kids, by life—and I didn't know what else to do.

I pinch my eyes shut, a string of curse words leaving my lips as I try to make sense of what's happening. How did we get here? How did I let things get this bad?

When I open my eyes again, Nick is still standing there, looking at me like he's waiting for an explanation I'm not sure I can give. His expression is unreadable, but there's something in his eyes—a mix of anger, frustration, and something else, something deeper I can't quite place.

"You should have told me," he says finally, his voice breaking through the silence.

"I'm sorry," I whisper, the words feeling inadequate, empty. There's so much more I want to say, but I can't seem to find the right words. My throat feels tight, and I can feel the tears building behind my eyes, threatening to spill over.

"I asked you to be more honest with me, to stop bottling things up," Nick continues, his voice growing louder, more urgent. "And instead, you've been carrying all this resentment —*years' worth*—and I had no idea. I can't fix what I don't know is broken, Letty."

The rawness in his voice hits me hard, and I feel a sob rise in my chest, but I choke it back, biting my lip to keep from crying. He's right. He's so right, and I hate it. I hate that I've let things get this far. I've spent so long trying to hold everything together on my own, thinking I could just push through it without his help.

"You told me what was wrong with the house," Nick continues, his voice softening. "You pointed out all the problems, and we fixed them together. You thought Sam wasn't taking care of himself properly, and you made sure to fix that too. You knew you were working too many hours and needed to pull back, and you did something about it. But when it comes to us, when it comes to our marriage, you couldn't give it the same attention. You couldn't even talk to me about it. You just wrote it down and stuffed it in a drawer."

His words are like daggers, each one piercing deeper than the last. I feel the weight of his disappointment, the frustration building inside him for months. And I don't know what to say. I don't know how to make it better.

"I wanted to fix things," I say finally, my voice barely above a whisper. "I thought...I thought I could handle it on my own."

Nick's face softens, and for the first time, I see the hurt in his eyes. The real, deep hurt I've caused by keeping him at arm's length, by trying to shoulder everything alone.

"You don't have to handle everything by yourself, Letty," he says quietly. "That's not how marriage works. We're supposed to be a team. We're supposed to face things together, no matter how hard they are. But you've been shutting me out, and I don't know how to fix that."

His words hit me like a punch to the gut, and the tears I've been holding back finally spill over. I sink to the floor, my body shaking with sobs as the weight of everything crashes down on me all at once. I've been trying so hard to be strong, to keep everything together, but in the process, I've pushed Nick away. I've forgotten what it means to be a partner, to rely on someone else when things get tough.

Nick kneels beside me, his hand resting gently on my shoulder, but he doesn't say anything. He just stays there, his presence comforting in its simplicity. I cry until there's nothing left, until I'm empty and exhausted, the weight of it all finally lifting, if only slightly.

"I'm sorry," I whisper again, my voice hoarse from crying. "I'm so sorry, Nick."

I should have thrown the list away as soon as I'd written it. No—I should never have written it in the first place. The idea I've become the type of person who would ever write such a list is something I'll need to face, along with the stark realization it's taken me until this very moment to understand I'm the problem here. Not my kids, not Nick, not Zoey, or work. I'm the unruly, unhappy, unsatisfied common denominator. I'm what needs fixing the most.

I can't fix what I don't know is broken, he said.

I'm what's broken.

"I know," he says softly, his hand gently squeezing my shoulder.

I'm what's broken, I tell myself again.

———

The following Monday morning, I find Nick in the kitchen, pouring his coffee for the road. He looks tired, but there's a softness in his expression that wasn't there before. It's like the tension between us has eased, even if only slightly. He glances up when I walk in, offering me a small smile.

I hesitate for a moment, unsure of how to approach him. But then I take a deep breath and walk over to him, letting my hand rest on his back. It's a small gesture, but it feels like a step in the right direction. Nick looks over his shoulder at me, his smile widening slightly.

"How would you feel about seeing a couple's counselor?" I ask, my voice soft, but steady. It's been on my mind for days, and I finally feel ready to bring it up.

Nick's eyebrows lift in surprise, and for a moment, he just stares at me like he's trying to figure out if I'm serious. Eventually, he nods. "I'm not against it," he says slowly. "But I think there's work we could be doing at home first. Together."

He pulls a small cooler bag from the pantry, and I watch as he packs his lunch—a leftover piece of lasagna and a few baby carrots the kids refused to touch. The sight is so mundane, so familiar, but it feels like a tiny step toward normalcy. Toward something better.

"I've been thinking a lot," Nick continues, his voice quiet but firm. "Since that night…since I found the list. And once I got over the anger, I started to see things more clearly. I can see why you were feeling the way you were."

I nod, my heart aching with guilt. "I'm sorry," I whisper. "I should have told you sooner. I should have been more open."

Nick sets his cooler down on the counter and steps closer, wrapping his arms around me. "I'll be better," he says softly, his voice thick with emotion. "I'll be better for you. For our family."

"I love you," I whisper, the words catching in my throat. I lean forward and kiss him.

"I love you too," Nick says, and for the first time in a long while, I believe him. I believe that we can fix this, that we can find our way back to each other. He smiles and heads for the door, greeting the kids as they come bounding down the stairs. "I'll let you know when I have an idea what time I'll be home."

Thank you, I mouth. And I am.

Ben is already dressed, his hair slicked back with water—his newest thing. "Can we go, Mom?" I smile down at him, wishing I could bottle up his excitement and sip from it whenever I need a pick-me-up. Who needs caffeine when you can drink up a toddler's enthusiasm for playtime?

To guarantee a few hours of focused work that morning

with camp now over, I've arranged a playdate for Ben with a kid a couple of blocks over. Trying to lean into encouraging Anna's independence, I leave her home while I walk Ben to his friend's place. It's hot and sticky despite the early hour, and by the time Ben arrives for his playdate, we're both sweaty and flushed. I kiss him goodbye at the door, promising to be back in three hours to pick him up, and then run home.

After a quick shower and a change of clothes, I'm at my desk, ready to come up with a plan to accomplish eight hours of work in four hours each day.

At first, it's hard trying to establish where my time is most valuable, but the deeper I dive, the easier it becomes. I can step back from writing cover copy, for example. And while I find the process of performing keyword research interesting, this is also something that can easily be assigned elsewhere. Same with writing website copy. Where I'm needed most is on the production side, vetting submissions, onboarding and managing our authors, setting due dates and release dates, and managing each manuscript as it moves through the editorial process. This is where I prevail, where my patience, perseverance, and dedication shine brightest. This, I assure myself, I can accomplish in only four hours.

It's how best to fill the rest of my time outside of work I need to figure out.

———

Later that night, after I've tucked Ben into bed, I hear the front door creak open, and I know Nick's home. I rush to our bedroom, quickly washing my face, brushing my teeth, and slipping into something much less comfortable than what I've been wearing all day.

I arrange myself on the bed, my heart pounding in my

chest. When Nick steps into the room, his eyes widen in surprise, a slow smile spreading across his face.

"Let me shower real quick," he says, his voice low and teasing.

He's out of the shower in record time, his body still damp as he crosses the room toward me. I laugh and brush the water droplets from his skin, pulling him closer by the back of his neck.

I kiss him deeply, the taste of lasagna still faint on his lips, but I don't care. There's something more important happening between us now, something like a small step toward healing. And as we lose ourselves in each other, I let myself believe we can fix this, that we can find our way back —one kiss, one touch at a time.

CHAPTER
TWENTY-EIGHT

Morning comes far too quickly. I put off getting out of bed for as long as I can, relishing the feel and memory of the last nine hours. After our lovemaking last night, which left both of us out of breath and amazed, Nick and I spent hours talking. We talked about the kids, about work, about the list—ugh—about our dreams for the next ten years. How had I forgotten it's Nick's dream to retire by fifty-five? We haven't spoken that much or so honestly since the early days of our relationship. It feels good. It feels right. It feels freeing. And getting out of bed now feels a little like leaving that moment behind.

Nick isn't in a rush to start his day either. Instead, we lie there, smiling at each other like we're teenagers again. I can't remember the last time I felt this happy. I can't remember the last time I looked at my husband like this and felt so drawn to him, so—dare I say it—turned on. If we're really quiet and make it snappy, we could—

A knock at the door startles us both. Ben, not waiting for a reply, pushes the door open and stands there watching us. Nick and I share a knowing smile before he jumps to his feet and lifts Ben into the air.

"Let's get you some breakfast, bud."

I savor the quiet for just a moment more, and then I head downstairs, closing my housecoat around me. In the kitchen, Ben is sitting at the table with a plate of buttered waffles, his mouth already sticky with syrup. Nick slides a fresh cup of coffee across the counter to me. I run my hand slowly along his backside as a thank you, smiling when Anna groans behind us.

"Get a room," she says, sneering.

I give Nick's butt a little squeeze, just to rub salt in my daughter's wound, sneaking a sidelong glance at her to see if she's noticed. She has.

"It's good for you to see that your mom and dad love each other," I say.

Her face scrunches up. "I know, I know. I don't need to hear it again. Please."

"Mom," Ben says, doing a spectacular job of changing the subject, "How come we haven't seen Sam and Stella in so long?"

I freeze. "I'm not sure, honey." It isn't entirely untrue. Despite Zoey answering her phone the other week, we haven't been in contact for months, and I have no idea why, or how long it'll go on.

"Is Zoey mad at you?"

I pinch my eyes shut. "I don't know."

He cocks his head, studying me. "If you did something to hurt her, you should say you're sorry."

"I know, bud. That's a good idea."

Ben has only eaten a few bites of waffles. "Keep eating," I say, knowing very well I'll be eating them later, all cold and nearly hard as a rock.

Nick comes up beside me, leaning into me. "Have you tried calling her again?"

I shake my head.

"You should."

I sigh. "You should have heard her the other day, Nick. She sounded so annoyed with me. This can't just be about me going into her house and tidying up. There's got to be something more, right? For her to have forced so much distance between us? And to keep the kids away..." I feel the sting of oncoming tears. "To borrow words from someone very wise, I can't fix what I don't know is broken."

Nick presses his lips to my temple. "I know you're feeling lost without her. You've got to talk to her and make it right—for all our sakes."

My voice is a near-whisper. "I know."

His mouth is against my ear as he says, "We're okay, Letty. We'll *be* okay."

I turn and kiss him then because he's said exactly what I need to hear.

Six simple words, and he's released me from my guilt.

———

I'm not too proud to admit I employ mild stalking to track down Zoey. That morning, buoyed by Nick's encouragement, I work from the living room, my eyes darting back and forth between the screen on my lap and the front window, through which I have a partial view of Zoey's front walk. If she leaves her house, I'll see her. If anyone approaches her front door, I'll see them too.

What I hadn't accounted for is that she'd already left the house early this morning, so I'm more than surprised when her garage suddenly opens and her dark SUV pulls in. Before the garage door closes, I can just make out three sets of feet getting out of the SUV.

"Anna!" I call out. She appears what could have been anywhere from two to eight minutes later, having stopped springing to action the second I call like Ben still does—bless his heart. "I need you to do me a favor."

"What is it?"

"I need you to go across the street and ask Zoey if she has any coffee. Tell her we've run out."

"Isn't that a little pathetic? I don't even drink coffee. She'll see right through us."

I think about the phone conversation Zoey and I had the other week, the annoyance in her voice. I think of the last time I saw her, the way she told me, *You've got your own family to worry about. I don't need you getting involved in mine*, and the pain I felt deep inside knowing I can't just walk over there whenever I want, call her whenever I want.

"I have to try," I say. "Please, Anna."

She shrugs. "Fine."

I watch her go through a crack in the shutters, my breathing heavy. She takes her time, in no apparent rush to try and save my friendship with the best friend I've ever had. Finally, she's at the front door. Her finger presses the Ring doorbell. I can hear the familiar chime in my head. There's a beat, and then the door swings open and—

My heart bursts open at the sight of her. When I saw her that night on the street months ago, I was shocked by how thin she looked. But it was nothing compared to what I see now. She's still thin, overly so, but the way she carries herself—it's as though she's unsure how to move in her body, and that...isn't Zoey.

The Zoey I know is strong and carries herself with confidence and poise at all times. I've been envious of it our entire friendship. Even from my vantage point, I can see she hasn't been taking care of herself the way she used to: her wavy hair is just a little too frizzy, and her skin just a little too red.

She and Anna speak for a moment, and then Anna steps inside, the door closing behind her. I stare at it, waiting until more than a few minutes have passed. Then, I begrudgingly go back to work.

Forty-five minutes later, which may as well have been weeks, Anna comes through the door. She takes one look at my face and screws up her own. "Chill, Mom. She invited me in for breakfast."

I continue to stare at her, at which point she produces a sealed bag of coffee and hands it to me. "She said it's your favorite."

Time seems to still as I look down at the floral packaging, studying the label. Mikava "Gesha Marsella." Zoey and I discovered the brand together, by accident, in a twist of fate. On a short vacation in Portland a couple of years ago, we went in search of a popular coffee shop we'd seen on Instagram, only to get lost and happen upon this little hole-in-the-wall café serving Mikava coffee that week as a promotional stunt. Neither of us thought it was the kind of place that would do such a thing but intrigued by the idea of a ten-dollar cup of coffee, we ordered two and took a seat on the well-loved chairs scattered around the café. It was—there's simply no other way to say it—the best cup of coffee either of us had ever had. We'd been obsessed ever since. It's expensive and often hard to find, and I had no idea she even bought it anymore.

In the kitchen, I go about the process of making myself a cup using the French press, just the way Zoey taught me, and then I return to my place in the living room. I drink it slowly, savoring every sip. Every so often, I look out the window and across the street and think of—

An olive branch! It has to be. This coffee is too special, too meaningful to just be coffee.

The door opens before I even reach it. I walk right through it and into Zoey's open arms, where I stay until she pulls away. I wait for her to invite me inside. Instead, we stand in her doorway.

I want to let Zoey talk first, but I'm too excited to be here with her, too excited to have her back. There's so much happening in our lives that the other doesn't know about, and I want to fix it immediately.

I know just where to start.

"First off, I've missed you. Holy hell, have I missed you. Second, I want to apologize for how I was acting. You were right to call me out on my shit, Zo. I've been a mess. Nick and I have been going through it, but I think we're coming out the other si—"

"Colette, stop." Her open palm hits the door with a slap.

I stand completely still, staring at her. "What?"

"You haven't changed one bit! I thought if I spent some time away from you, I would calm down, maybe even get over what I've been feeling, but this is… You are…"

"I'm confused."

Zoey laughs bitterly. "You don't even know you do it, do you?"

"Do what?" I whisper.

She pauses, debating whether or not to answer. I have the feeling she's trying to decide how honest she wants to be.

"It's all about you! It's always all about you!" Her mouth screws up as though she's smelling something foul. "I'm sick of it. I've *been* sick of it."

I reach out to steady myself against the wall, my heart racing. An image suddenly comes to me. Zoey and Aaron smiling and flirting with each other as they unload groceries from the back of Zoey's SUV. It makes no sense, and I shake my head, attempting to rid my mind of it.

What are we talking about again?

"That's what I was trying to say, Zo. I'm a mess, and—"

"No, *I'm* a mess!" she says. There's pure venom in her tone. "You're just tired and unhappy like the rest of 'em."

I'm silent, my mind whirling.

"I keep giving you all these chances, hoping you'll realize how you sound, but nope—it's the same sad song on repeat."

"What chances? What are you even talking about?"

"My husband had an affair, Letty. My marriage—my whole life—has been an absolute mess for over five months, and all you can talk about is you! I kept brushing it under the rug, hoping you'd come around, but you just keep letting me down. I don't need that on top of everything else going on. I don't need—"

I've been staring at the floor, but now I look up.

Me. She's going to say she doesn't need me.

"I've been trying to talk to you for weeks, but you just cut me out of your life like I'm nothing."

"You still don't get it."

"I'm here now. Can't we just move on?" I ask quietly. "I came to apologize for everything I may have said or done to upset you. We can talk about whatever you want."

"But you didn't actually say 'I'm sorry,' did you?"

I close my eyes. This is not going as I hoped. Again.

"I'm sorry, Zo. I'll do better."

I watch my best friend of over ten years slowly shake her head. "I can't keep doing this. I have no interest in one-sided friendships at my age. We're too old for this shit."

I reach for her hands, taking both of them in mine, and look straight into her eyes. "I'm so sorry. Please forgive me. Tell me what to do to fix this, and I'll do it."

Zoey looks down at our intertwined hands and then back

at me. I watch her mouth open and close. My heart seems to have stopped beating as it waits for her response.

"I'm sorry," I say once again. And then I say the only thing I can think to say at this moment, the only thing that matters. "Tell me what's happening with you. Tell me what's going on with Aaron. I promise I'm here to listen."

CHAPTER
TWENTY-NINE

They went about the whole thing wrong—or so Zoey says—as she finally invites me inside. I hesitate on the threshold for a moment, catching the expression in her eyes, a mix of exhaustion and wariness. This isn't going to be easy, for either of us.

Once inside, she offers me another cup of coffee, and I'm grateful for the familiar gesture. It feels like a small step toward normalcy, but it's a hollow kind of normal. As the coffee brews, Zoey stands by the counter, staring into space, her hands resting on the edge of the sink. There's a tension in her posture, the kind of exhaustion that doesn't come from lack of sleep but from carrying an invisible burden for too long. I want to say something—anything—to ease the weight pressing down on her, but I hold back, unsure if my words would help or hurt.

When we finally sit down on her couch, mugs in hand, Zoey sends Sam and Stella over to my place to hang with Anna and Ben, their voices fading as they rush out the door. The house falls silent, and it's just the two of us.

For a long moment, Zoey doesn't speak. She just stares at her coffee cup, tracing the rim with her finger, her face etched with worry. I can tell she's thinking about how to start, about how much to tell me, how much to hold back. The air between us feels heavy and fragile. I wait, heart in my throat, wanting her to know whatever she says, I'm here. I always will be.

Finally, she takes a deep breath. "The night you took the kids..." Her voice cracks slightly, and she hesitates, long enough for me to see how much recalling that memory hurts her. I almost want to call the whole thing off. Maybe this is too much for her. But before I can suggest we leave it for another day, she continues.

"It was terrible, Letty. Just awful." She swallows hard. "Aaron made dinner. I don't even remember what it was—just that there were dishes everywhere, and he'd never made it before. He was trying so hard, and it was actually pretty good, but all I could think about was *where* he learned to make it. Was it something she made for him? Did *she* teach him?"

Her voice wavers, and my heart aches for her. I can see the pain etched into every line of her face, and it's like I'm feeling it, too. The idea of sitting there, eating a meal tasting of betrayal, of wondering where her husband learned how to cook for another woman, makes me want to scream for her. My hands grip the mug tighter, imagining how I would feel in her place—every bite must have felt like swallowing poison.

"I tried to keep eating," she continues, her voice quieter now, more broken. "But once the thought got in my head, I couldn't choke it down. I couldn't even look at him. That's when it all started to unravel."

I watch her closely, trying to read the emotions flitting across her face—anger, sorrow, regret. Zoey isn't someone who unravels easily, and seeing her like this makes me feel helpless, useless even. For years, she had been my rock, always knowing what to say, always steady. And now, she's the one breaking apart, and I'm the one who doesn't know how to hold her together.

"I didn't want to know," she says, her voice barely above a whisper. "I told you before, remember? I didn't want the details. I didn't want to know how long it had been going on, where they'd met, who made the first move. But I couldn't stop myself. I asked him everything. Every little nagging question that had been plaguing me."

I swallow hard, my fingers tightening around my mug. *How much does one person have to endure before they break?*

"Her name was Eve," Zoey says after a long pause, her lips curling into a bitter smile. "She made the first move apparently. He says he didn't think anything of it at first. She worked at this bar where people from his office went sometimes, and I've even been there with him, but I never noticed her. He says she was just being friendly. But as time went on, she got more flirty, and he liked the attention."

Zoey's smile fades, and her eyes glisten with unshed tears. "And I get it," she says, her voice shaking slightly. "I *understand*, because I felt the same way with that waiter, remember? But it still hurt, Letty. It still felt like a knife to the gut when he admitted it. If we'd just been more honest with each other, maybe none of this would've happened."

Her words hit me hard, and I reach out, placing my hand over hers. I don't know what to say. I want to comfort her, to tell her it's not her fault, that no one can predict or prevent these things, but I know it's not so simple. Life is messy, and relationships—even the strongest ones—can be so fragile.

"Zo..."

She doesn't look at me, her gaze fixed on the floor. "He was drunk the first time they slept together. But not the second, or the third, or any time after. He knew what he was doing. He said he got really good at separating his life into two parts. When he was home with me and the kids, he could switch off the other side of his life—like it didn't even exist. But when he was with her…"

Zoey's voice trails off, and I can see the weight of the betrayal still sits heavily on her shoulders, even if she's had time to process it. The sheer pain of it must have been unbearable, and yet, here she is—telling me, facing it head-on. I feel a surge of anger rise in my chest, hot and fierce. "I'm going to kill him," I say, the words slip out before I can stop them.

Zoey smiles, but it's a sad, defeated smile. "I felt that way too, at first. But now… I don't know. Maybe I've had enough distance from it, or maybe I've just spent too many nights obsessing over it, but I can see where we both went wrong."

I nod, though I'm not sure I could be as gracious as she is. I admire her strength, even if I don't understand it. I'm not sure I ever could, or if I'd have the same grace to face something like this with such clarity. There's no telling how I'd react if I were in her shoes and it terrifies me.

"We didn't get much accomplished that first night," she continues. "I cried, he cried. There was a lot of yelling. It was intense but at the end of it, I told him he had to leave. It was three in the morning, and I was exhausted. I couldn't even look at him."

I remember the morning she came to pick up the twins, the way she appeared so hollow, so broken. I had wanted to ask her how things had gone but the dullness in her eyes kept me from saying a word. I wonder if she knew I had been watching her, waiting for some sign, some hint of what had happened. It's strange how we think we know someone's story just by looking at them, but we never really know the full truth. And I hadn't pushed—I had been afraid of hurting her more.

"We didn't talk for a while after that," Zoey says, her voice taking on a faraway tone. "I needed space. I told him I'd call when I was ready, but until then, I didn't want to hear from him. And for a while, all I did was cry. It felt like I couldn't stop. Every time I thought I was done, the tears would start again."

I can imagine it—Zoey curled up on the couch, clutching a pillow, her body racked with sobs. The image makes my heart hurt. The idea of her going through this all alone, with no one to share her pain, crushes me.

She looks at me then, her eyes full of sadness. "People started to find out. They'd text or call, but it wasn't really about me or the kids. They just wanted the gossip, the drama. They wanted to know if I had suspected anything. It made me feel like I couldn't trust anyone, not even my own thoughts. And that's why I pushed you away, Letty. It wasn't about you. It was about me needing space from *everything*."

Her words hit me like a wave, crashing over me, pulling me under. All this time, I thought she had pushed me away because I wasn't enough. Because I had failed her. But it was never only about me.

"I should have just told you," Zoey continues. "I know you would've given me space if I asked, but I couldn't even trust myself to ask for it. I didn't know what I needed."

"It's okay, Zo," I say softly. "I get it now. I was so caught up in my own issues that I didn't realize what was happening with you. I'm sorry I wasn't there when you needed me."

Her expression softens, and for the first time in a long while, I see a flicker of the old Zoey. The one who always knew what to say, who could make me laugh even when I didn't want to. The one who, for years, had been my rock.

"Aaron stayed away for a while after that," she says, shifting the conversation back to him. "But then he started lingering when he'd drop off the kids. It was like he wanted to be around, even if it was just for a few minutes in the driveway. He didn't push me for answers or beg me to take him back. He just…stayed."

"That's sweet," I say, though I can hear the hesitation in my own voice. It's hard to feel happy for Aaron after everything he's done, but I can see what it means to Zoey, so I don't press it.

"He eventually told me he'd found a place to live, a short-term lease. I knew what he wanted me to say—that he should come home. But I wasn't ready. I'm still not sure if I am."

I swallow hard, the question burning on my tongue. "Do you still want to be with him?"

Zoey exhales deeply, setting her coffee mug down on the table. "For a while, I didn't. I thought that chapter of my life was over, that I'd never be able to look at him without feeling hurt. But something's changed."

She pauses, her fingers twisting in her lap. I can see the internal battle waging inside her, the constant push and pull between love and betrayal, between hope and despair. It's a battle I know all too well, and my heart aches for her.

"I realized I wasn't grieving the loss of our marriage, but the loss of what it *used* to be," she continues, her voice steady but soft. "Our marriage can never be what it once was, but that doesn't mean it's over. It just means it has to be something new, something different."

Her words hang in the air between us, and I feel a strange sense of understanding wash over me. What she's saying resonates with something deep inside me. Marriage, relationships—they evolve. They change, and sometimes, they break. But it doesn't always mean they're beyond repair. It just means they need to be rebuilt, redefined.

"So…where do you stand now?" I ask, my voice barely above a whisper. I'm almost afraid to hear the answer, but I need to know. I need to understand where she is in all of this.

Zoey looks down at her hands for a long moment, her

thumb rubbing absently over the edge of her wedding ring. Finally, she meets my eyes, and there's a flicker of hope in her gaze that wasn't there before. "We're not together. Not yet. But we're talking. And for the first time in a long time, I can look at him and not want to scream. That's a start."

I nod, feeling a flicker of relief. There's no saying what the future holds for Zoey and Aaron, or for Nick and me, but for the first time in a long while, I feel a sense of hope. Maybe we can all find our way back, in time. Maybe, just maybe, things don't have to stay broken forever.

Zoey takes a deep breath, leaning back on the couch. She looks tired, but there's something lighter about her now, like she's finally starting to shed the weight of the last few months. "But enough about me," she says, her voice softer now. "How are you and Nick doing?"

The question catches me off guard. For a moment, I don't know how to answer. How *are* Nick and I doing? After everything we've been through—the fights, the silence, the long stretches of disconnection—I'm not sure where we stand.

But as I sit there, thinking about the night before—how we'd finally talked, really talked, and how we'd made love like we hadn't in years—I realize, despite everything, we're still fighting for each other. We're still in this, even if we're not sure how to fix it.

"We're...trying," I say, my voice tentative. "It hasn't been easy, and there are still a lot of things we need to work through. But last night, we finally had a real conversation. We opened up about a lot of things we've been avoiding for years. And for the first time in a long time, it felt like we were on the same team again."

Zoey smiles, a small, encouraging smile making me feel a little less lost. "That's good, Letty."

I shrug, feeling a wave of uncertainty wash over me. "I don't know. It's a start, I guess. But there's still so much unresolved. I mean, we've been distant for so long, and I'm not sure how to bridge the gap. Sometimes it feels like we're both walking on eggshells, afraid to say or do the wrong thing. And then there's the house…God, the house. It's like a literal representation of everything wrong between us."

Zoey raises an eyebrow. "The house?"

I laugh, but it's a bitter, tired sound. "Yeah, the renovations. It's been this constant source of tension for us. I wanted to move, but Nick insisted on staying and fixing the place up. We started the renovations thinking it would bring us closer together, but it's only highlighted how far apart we really are. Every unfinished project, every unpainted wall, it's like a reminder of all the things we haven't fixed in our marriage."

Zoey nods, her expression thoughtful. "I get it. But you know, Letty, the house doesn't have to be perfect for you guys to be okay. Maybe it's more about learning to live with the imperfections, both in the house and in your relationship."

Her words hit me harder than I expected. Maybe she's right. Maybe I've been so focused on trying to fix everything —Nick, the house, our marriage—that I've lost sight of the fact some things don't need to be perfect to work. Maybe it's okay to live in the mess for a while, to let things be unfinished, and trust we'll figure it out together.

"I never thought about it like that," I admit, feeling a small sense of relief wash over me. "I've been so obsessed with fixing everything I forgot how to just…be. Maybe that's what Nick and I need. To stop trying to fix each other and just start being honest, even if it's messy."

Zoey smiles warmly, making me feel a little less alone. "It's not easy, Letty. But you'll get there. You and Nick—you're strong. You've made it through a lot. You can make it through this, too."

For the first time in a long time, I believe her.

As we sit there in the quiet of her living room, sipping our coffee, I realize that maybe we're both on the same journey. We're both trying to find our way back to the people we love, trying to figure out how to rebuild something broken. And maybe, just maybe, we'll find our way back to each other, too.

The silence between us isn't uncomfortable anymore. It's full of unspoken understanding, of shared pain and hope. And for the first time since all of this started, I feel like we're going to be okay.

Zoey glances at me, her eyes soft but curious. "You know, it's funny…after everything that's happened, I didn't think I'd ever be able to talk about this with anyone, let alone you. But I'm glad we're here. I'm glad we're talking."

I nod, my throat tight with emotion. "Me too, Zo. Me too."

As I leave Zoey's house later that afternoon, I feel lighter than I have in weeks. The road ahead is still uncertain, but for the first time in a long while, I'm not walking it alone.

CHAPTER
THIRTY

Nick finds me in the office that night, finishing up some work I didn't get done during the work day. The light from my computer screen is the only illumination in the room, casting a soft glow over the papers and notebooks scattered across my desk. I feel a slight tension in my shoulders, but it's nothing compared to what I've been carrying for the last few months. Tonight, though, it feels like a weight has been lifted.

"You look like you've won the lottery," Nick says as he leans against the doorframe, his familiar presence warming the room.

"I feel like I have," I say, my fingers pausing on the keyboard. I turn to look at him, a real, unforced smile tugging at my lips. "Mending things with Zoey…it's like a huge weight has been lifted off me. I didn't realize just how much I was carrying until now."

"I'm glad," Nick says, his voice soft. He crosses the room, bending down to kiss the top of my head. Sometimes I forget just how tall he is, how his simple presence can make me feel safe, like maybe we can work through our issues. "I'll get dinner started," he offers, his tone gentle, as though he's in tune with my relief.

My eyes dart to the clock at the top of my computer screen. Somehow, it's already six p.m. The hours slipped by unnoticed, absorbed by work and the lingering emotional release from earlier. "It's not like the kids to not have bugged me for something by now," I say, a little surprised.

Nick mumbles in agreement before closing the door behind him. His departure leaves a calm quiet in the room, but as I sit back in my chair, I realize I can't focus. My mind is buzzing, not with stress or work, but with the feeling of possibility—like maybe I can fix things, maybe things can be good again.

I try to push through, working a little longer, but eventually, fueled by the incredible smell wafting in from the kitchen, I give up and shut down my computer. As I sit in the now-quiet office, I feel something I haven't felt in a long time —hope. I need to learn to be comfortable with knowing I won't be able to accomplish everything as quickly as I want to. But that's part of the point of shortening my hours. I'm shortening the list of expectations placed on me in hopes I can fix what's most broken—myself.

I walk into the kitchen, the smell of garlic and butter filling the air, and find Nick already plating dinner. He's humming softly to himself, and for a brief moment, everything feels...normal.

Over a dinner of chicken fettuccine and some of the most lethal homemade garlic bread I've ever come across, I decide to fill the kids in on our plan for the foreseeable future.

"I wanted to talk to you guys about something," I say, glancing between Anna and Ben. Anna is twirling her pasta on her fork, her focus more on the food than me, but Ben's wide eyes are glued to my face. Without a phone at the table to distract her, it's much easier to hold Anna's interest. "I'm sure you've noticed Dad has been working a lot more hours lately."

"Mm-hmm," Ben says, nodding seriously as though he's been taking careful note of Nick's comings and goings. I stifle a smile.

"Well, he and Will are doing really well, so they've decided to take on more jobs. And while that means Dad is going to be extra busy for a while, it allows me to scale back at work, should I want to."

"What's that mean?" Ben asks, his voice small but curious. He looks so sweet and innocent. I wish, not for the first time, that I could bottle it up and keep it all to myself.

"It means that in a couple of weeks, I'm going to be dropping back to part-time hours. Which means I'll be available to all of you more."

Ben's face lights up immediately, his fork abandoned on his plate. "Will you still be able to drive us to school?"

"Of course."

"And pick us up?"

"Definitely."

"And will you still pack my lunches in the morning?"

I smile, reaching out to brush a lock of hair from his face. "Absolutely."

"Then I say go for it," Ben says, a broad smile stretching across his face, as if this was the most important decision of the day.

I meet Nick's eyes across the table. He's smiling widely, his gaze full of approval and something else—something I haven't seen in a long time. Pride.

Anna, on the other hand, is quiet. She studies me and Nick carefully, as though she's trying to figure out if there's more to this announcement than what I've said.

"What are you thinking, Banana?" I ask, using her old nickname in a gentle attempt to draw her out.

"You'll be more available," she says, more of a statement than a question. Her eyes narrow slightly, but not in suspicion —more like she's processing the idea.

"Mm-hm." I wait, knowing there's more to her comment. Best to let her get to it at her own pace.

I keep eating, stealing glances at her from the corner of my eye. I watch her stab her fork into the food, twirl the pasta around it, and push it into her mouth. I watch her watch me, too, from the corner of her eye. It feels like we're both waiting for the other to say something that will break the silence.

Finally, Anna sets down her fork and says, "Do you think maybe we could go back to running after school?"

I'm so surprised by the request I almost drop my fork. Easy, I tell myself. Don't scare her away. She'll turn and run in the other direction never to be found again.

"I think it's a great idea," I say, my heart thumping in my chest. Running after school had been our thing once—before everything else got in the way.

"Could we listen to the podcast I heard you and Zoey talking about? The one where people submit their love stories?" she asks, her voice tentative, like she's afraid I'll say no.

It takes me a moment to remember what she's referring to. The *Modern Love* podcast. It's not something I thought she'd be interested in, but the fact she's suggesting it gives me hope. "I think we could arrange that," I say, smiling.

And just as I'm imagining all the quality time I'm going to get to spend with my daughter, all the chances to have a real conversation with her, all the love and respect that will balloon and grow until we've developed the kind of mother-daughter relationship I always hoped we'd have, she goes and says something to bring me right back down to earth.

"Don't go turning into one of those moms at school whose life revolves around looking cute in athleisurewear and carting their kids to and from activities," she says, her tone half serious, half teasing. "Nicki's mom has absolutely nothing to do all day except work out and drive her crazy trying to get all up in her business. It's so embarrassing."

I stifle a laugh. "Okay, Anna." I hold my right hand over my heart. "I solemnly swear I am up to no good."

She smirks, rolling her eyes. "That makes no sense, but ten points for referencing *Harry Potter*."

Anna stands up and takes her empty dish to the sink, where she rinses it and puts it in the dishwasher. Then, she turns to us, leaning against the counter, her arms crossed.

"Does this mean you're going to be less stressed out?" she asks, her expression suddenly serious.

Nick glances at me, a small smile playing on his lips.

"I'm sorry if my stress level with work was affecting you," I say, my voice softening. "I do try to keep work stuff to myself, but it's like we always tell you kids: I'm only human and I'm not perfect. I'm going to make mistakes," I say. I make eye contact with both of them before continuing. "But I will always, always, try to do better and be better…for you, and for Ben."

Ben, being the adorable, lovely child he so often is, blows me a kiss from across the table, his eyes twinkling with affection. Then, he looks down at his plate, still mostly full of fettuccine, and pushes it away with a sigh.

Some things, I'm afraid, will never change.

The following morning, I open an email Brent sent late the night before. It's brief, but it sends a wave of unease through me: Give me a call when you log on this morning. A call, not a huddle or Zoom, but an actual phone call.

Brent and I don't talk on the telephone. We haven't since I

first applied for the position ten years ago. I can't help but feel the weight of this change in communication as I stare at the message, my stomach tightening with nervous anticipation. I take a deep breath, pull up his contact information, and press the call button, my heart thumping louder with each ring.

Brent picks up after the first ring, his voice buzzing with the energy of a man who's likely already consumed three cups of coffee. "I'm going to jump right in since I know you're busy," he says in his usual brisk, no-nonsense way. It's his standard opening line. "Now that you've had some time to think since our last conversation—"

Time to think? It's been five days since I told him I'd be cutting back my hours. Five chaotic days filled with Zoey, Nick, the kids, and trying to figure out how to make sense of everything. *Time to think* feels like a luxury I haven't been afforded, but I let him continue without interruption.

"I wanted to know if your decision to cut back your hours is because you're not feeling challenged enough?"

I blink, taken aback by the question. "If you're asking if I have plans to leave, the answer is no."

"I'm glad to hear it," Brent says, but I can sense there's more coming. "I wanted to talk to you this morning before you've fully made up your mind about minimizing your hours." He clears his throat, and I can already tell he's about to make a pitch. "It's recently come to my attention that there's a hole in the management team, a space needing to be filled. I think you'd be perfect for it. You've been with the company almost from the beginning, and you know it inside and out. If it's a challenge you need, or something with a little more autonomy and authority, this is it."

I'm grateful Brent can't see my face so he can't witness the visceral reaction I'm having to his words.

He adds, "Your salary would be significantly higher, too, if it's of any concern."

I close my eyes and count to three before responding. "Brent," I say, my voice sharper than I intended. I take another breath, softening my tone. "It's not about the money, it's not about the autonomy or authority. It's a personal decision based on what's right for me and my family right now."

There's a pause, and I can almost see him sitting there, probably tapping his fingers on his desk, his mind working to find another angle. "What if—"

"Brent," I cut him off gently, but firmly. "I'm very grateful for the opportunity, and maybe it's something we can talk about six months or even a year down the line, but right now my mind is made up. I just can't take it on at the moment."

There's another pause, longer this time. I know him well enough to know he's not happy. He's never been good at accepting no for an answer. "Okay," he says finally, but I know it isn't really.

We exchange a few minor pleasantries before ending the call. I sit there for a moment, staring at the phone in my hand, feeling a strange mixture of relief and doubt. Brent's retirement plans have been on the horizon for a while now, and I know he's been grooming me to take on more responsibility, to one day run the whole show. But the thought of stepping into those shoes feels...wrong.

I know without a doubt it's not what I want.

———

Later, as I settle into bed, Nick is beside me, a book resting in his lap. I'm messing around on my laptop, not doing anything important, just mindlessly scrolling. I glance at him, his profile calm and composed, his expression softened by the glow of the bedside lamp.

"He's scared to lose you," Nick says suddenly, breaking the comfortable silence. His eyes don't leave his book, but there's a knowing edge to his voice. "Now that the writing's on the wall, he's scared of what it says."

I stare at him for a moment, processing his words. "Maybe," I say quietly, turning my attention back to my laptop, though I can't focus.

The truth is, I'm done obsessing over work. I've been doing it for far too many years, and it hasn't gotten me where I want to be. One of the best things I can do for myself now is to let go of what no longer serves me. Obsessing over things I can't control? That's one of them.

I close my laptop with a soft click and set it aside on the nightstand. "I was thinking I might take up yoga," I say, the thought slipping out before I've fully thought it through.

Nick's eyes widen in surprise, and then a slow smile spreads across his face. "I thought you said you aren't graceful enough for yoga."

The image of Zac briefly flickers in my mind—how his comment about me finding my own thing had planted the seed. I push it away, grateful to have come to my senses before things went too far. "I figure it'll come with practice," I say with a shrug, leaning back against the pillows.

Nick shifts in bed, turning toward me. His book falls from his lap and onto the floor with a soft thud. He watches me silently for a moment, his gaze warm and thoughtful, and I can see something playful flickering behind his eyes.

"What?" I ask, raising an eyebrow.

His lips twitch into a grin, and his eyes take on a mischievous glint. "I'm just picturing you in all that tight clothing..." He wiggles his eyebrows suggestively and bites his bottom lip. "I approve of your choice of extracurricular activity."

I roll my eyes and slap at him playfully, but my hand lingers on his chest. His mouth finds mine, soft and warm, and before I know it, the playful teasing is replaced with something deeper, something that makes my heart race.

There's nothing playful about what happens next. The tension of the day, the relief of mending things with Zoey, the release of choosing myself for once—it all culminates in this moment. It feels like we're finding our way back to each other, piece by piece.

CHAPTER
THIRTY-ONE

Nick comes home long after dinner has been cooked, served, and cleaned up, long after Ben has been tucked in. Some nights, Anna stays up with me, waiting for him to come home, just wanting to see him walk through the front door, but most nights, the house is quiet by 9 p.m. On these nights, when a book or show fails to entertain me, my overthinking begins in earnest.

Some nights, I think about how my life might look to people on the outside—like the young woman in line behind me at the grocery store the day before, who does a terrible job pretending she isn't staring at me. I want to be annoyed, but I can't blame her. There was a time in my life when I watched women like me—older, married with children—with an extreme sense of curiosity, wondering what their life was like, sometimes dreaming of it being my own one day.

What did she think when she looked at me? What conclusions did she draw from the dark circles under my eyes, the way I spoke to Ben, the way my daughter ignored me whenever I asked her a question? Did she lose interest and turn away, or watch long enough to see the next moment—when

Ben told me he loved me out of the blue, or Anna leaned over to show me a funny video on her phone? When she looked at me, did she see just a mother, a wife, a woman approaching forty? Or did she look deeper—the way I've learned you must when looking at anyone else's life from the outside?

Zoey's life had looked perfect from the outside, but it was revealed to be far from it. And my life, as imperfect as it has always been, feels like it's only now just taking the shape it was meant to all along.

True to form, I'm thinking about all this as I lie in bed on a Tuesday night in early August, waiting for Nick to come home. It's been the kind of smooth, easy day that catches you off guard, leaving you feeling like you can take on the world. Like Ben's moments of sweet innocence, I want to bottle up this feeling to save for a rainy day. It certainly comes in handy when, only thirty minutes later, Nick walks into the bedroom, looking glum.

"You look tired," I say gently. There are slight bags under his eyes, and his shoulders are drooped. I know the look all too well. His long workdays are catching up with him. As he showers, I wonder if he ever fantasizes about finding a way out of the chaos, about blowing up his life as he knows it—as I once did, as so many of us have.

He comes out of the bathroom a few minutes later. I've turned off most of the lights, casting the room in a dull glow. "That feels better," he says. He gives Mayer a scratch behind the ears and then lies down beside me on the bed. I sense, as I sometimes do with the kids when they mill around me, that Nick has something he wants to say.

He says nothing for so long I wonder if he's fallen asleep. I turn to face him, and he stirs.

"Is there anything else I need to know about?" he eventually asks, looking down at my arm, running his fingertips lazily up and down my forearm. "Anything you didn't add to the list?"

I grimace, but Nick smiles.

"What I want is to never speak of the list again," I say. "Can we do that?"

He leans forward and kisses me softly, his next words spoken against my mouth. "I think that can be arranged."

I look at him then—those irresistible light eyes of his—and wonder when it was I stopped really seeing him. He's never gone anywhere; he's always been right here in front of me, all these years. Right from the beginning.

How did I, just months ago, go so long feeling like I had to go it alone, to be alone in my experience?

Here's a man who, fourteen years ago, said "I do" and promised to love me through thick and thin. While we've had our share of ups and downs, he's still here with me. He continues to choose me, day after day. And despite our differences, he still does.

People enter marriage for myriad reasons. Maybe they want to feel secure or less lonely. Maybe they marry for financial or religious reasons or because they feel pressured by society. I had expectations about what my marriage would look like, and I'm certain Nick did too, but I failed to remember one indisputable fact: I wasn't alone. And I didn't ever have to be.

Not unless I choose to be.

———

Like many wives, mothers, and parents, I'm tired, and I've spent too much time pretending to be okay with that. Pretending has become second nature. I tell myself stories about being too busy. I tell myself I'm not happy. I tell myself it's all out of my control.

I think about all this as I sit in an oversized wicker chair in my best friend's backyard, watching our children splash in the pool. Their laughter echoes in the late summer air, the kind of sound you want to etch into your memory.

Next to the pool, Aaron hovers over a large grill, a thin string of smoke rising into the air. Soon, there will be hamburgers and hot dogs to be eaten, lemonade thick with sugar to be drunk, and watermelon that'll leave our hands sticky and sweet. I turn and watch Zoey emerge from the back door, her hands full of condiments, which she sets on the patio table next to the grill. My eyes immediately go to Aaron, who watches her from the corner of his eye with open adoration. Zoey catches him looking and smiles shyly. I smile down at my lap.

July has been hot, but August is even warmer. I adjust my position in the chair and wipe a line of sweat from my forehead. I look longingly at the pool. I may have picked up a new hobby and started being more open about what I want from my husband, but I haven't yet managed to quiet the little voice in the back of my head complaining about my aging body.

Baby steps.

Zoey approaches me, holding two margaritas, one of which she hands to me. She sits down next to me with a satisfied sigh. "The end of summer, already," she says wistfully.

The summer—the year, really—has moved in slowly and then disappeared in the blink of an eye. I'm ready, however, for the new season, for the next chapter to begin. I have a pretty good idea of how it's going to turn out.

We sip our drinks, Zoey watching Aaron, me watching her watch Aaron.

"I used to compare my marriage to yours constantly, you know," I say.

She smiles and rolls her eyes. "Silly Colette. Bet you know better now."

My gaze bounces from her to the kids and back again. "There's still so much love here in this home. I feel it every time I'm here, every time I'm around the two of you. If that's what you want, you'll find your way back to each other."

Zoey sucks in her bottom lip, looking at me over the tip of her glass. "He kissed me the other day," she says.

I lean in, rapt. "How did it feel?"

"Strange."

"I bet."

"I mean, at first, it was strange, but then it felt…normal. Natural."

Hope blooms in my chest. "I'm happy to hear that."

Zoey takes a long drink from her glass. "How are you and Nick doing?"

Against my better judgment or, really, my incessant inner monologue, I still believe Aaron and Zoey are models of a great marriage, one that can take a hit and survive. If they can make it, so can Nick and I.

"Better each day," I say. And it's the truth—no sugarcoating, no pretending.

She squints into the sunlight. "Where is he, by the way?"

I grin. "He's running a quick errand before dinner."

"Ugh." She turns away from me dramatically. "I'm never going to forgive you for leaving me, you know."

"Two miles is nothing," I say, though I know, deep down, our friendship will change when I'm no longer living just across the street. It will adapt to a new normal and perhaps even grow into something better and stronger.

Aaron approaches us and refills our drinks. I notice he fills Zoey's first, even though he's closer to me. The feeling of hope in my chest is about ready to explode.

"So the big day's tomorrow, huh?"

Zoey's frown makes me laugh. "Don't rub salt in the wound," she says.

"Nick's gone to pick up the U-Haul now so we can get started in the morning." I sip my margarita. "If it weren't my dream house we were moving into, I would have killed him for suggesting we move during the hottest month of the year."

"I want to kill him too, so we're in agreement," Zoey says. She holds up her glass, toasting us. "Moving away from me—you and your crazy ideas."

Nick suddenly appears next to me. "Our crazy ideas," he says, grinning. He takes my drink from my hand and drinks it down in its entirety.

Aaron refills his glass and then fetches me a drink of my own. Against the backdrop of our four children in the pool, we toast to the end of the summer, and new beginnings.

"And to the end of pretending," I add.

I turn away from Zoey and Aaron's smiling faces to look at Nick. I look straight into his beautiful eyes, feeling the now-familiar tug in the pit of my stomach. "I love you, you know."

He bends down to kiss me. "I love you, too."

Zoey jumps to her feet. "I almost forgot, I have something for you two." She's back almost as quickly as she's gone, carrying a dirty paper bag. "Here."

I look sidelong at Nick.

"Don't be like that," she says. "Just open it."

I'm already laughing as I pull out the bag of fertilizer. Somehow, impossibly, I've known what I'm going to find inside.

"It's for the grass at your new house," she says, grinning.

I look first to Nick, and then up at the bright blue Las Vegas sky.

I wish for rain.

A LOOK AT:
ELEANOR & SAM

A witty tale of ambition, friendship, and the delicate balance between chasing one's dreams while holding on to what matters most.

Eleanor Wild has it all—except for a single good idea.

As a bestselling author with a bad case of writer's block and a family on the brink of mutiny, Eleanor agrees to a family vacation in Las Vegas. But instead of relaxation, she finds herself sitting next to Sam Sutton, a twenty-three-year-old aspiring author with a knack for both storytelling and oversharing.

What starts as a mid-flight chat turns into an unlikely friendship, with Sam's raw enthusiasm and bold ideas sparking the creative fire Eleanor thought she'd lost forever. But as their collaboration takes off, so do the complications. Between her neglected family, Sam's growing resentment of her own struggling dreams, and a moral gray area that grows darker by the day, Eleanor's balancing act is starting to look more like a high-stakes gamble.

Set against the neon-lit chaos of Las Vegas, Eleanor & Sam explores the complexities of ambition, the struggle for balance, and the power of second chances—proving that what happens in Vegas doesn't always stay there…especially when it's your career and family on the line.

For fans of Writers & Lovers and Blank, this heartwarming and witty contemporary women's fiction tale offers a poignant look at the intersection of creativity, family, and self-discovery.

AVAILABLE NOW

ACKNOWLEDGMENTS

Thank you to my friends, support network, and early readers: Jordan Hansen, Suzy Krause, Dela Ballard, and Amanda VanOpdorp.

I started writing this book while in a brilliant mastermind run by Camille Pagán. To Camille, and the other wonderful women who took part, thank you for the guidance, comradery, and inspiration.

Thank you to my editor, Amy Briggs for pushing me to show more than tell.

To my husband, Dominic and son, DJ: I write because I have to, but also for you.

ABOUT THE AUTHOR

Rachel Del Grosso was born in Ontario, Canada. She began writing at a very young age, but has since learned to write in complete sentences. She writes fiction about love in the form of imperfect marriages, messy friendships, and complicated families. She lives in Las Vegas with her husband and son. *Another Kind of Green* is her third novel.

Find her on Instagram *@authorracheldelgrosso* and TikTok *@authorracheldelgrosso* and sign up for her newsletter at *racheldelgrosso.substack.com* or www.racheldelgrosso.com